As N
Necessary As Breathing.

Meg felt Lucas's start of surprise as her lips touched his, and then she was where she wanted to be, had needed to be, in an embrace that healed and filled all the empty caverns in her heart.

She felt the brush of the mat as he lowered her to it, felt the weight of Lucas against her, felt the tangle of their legs. She felt a need as Lucas took control of the kiss she'd begun.

Desire. Had she ever really felt it before?

And more. Much more. Every nerve ending she possessed had sprung to life, demanding… demanding something she'd never believed in until this moment.

Had anyone ever *cherished* her—because she could only have dreamed of this happening, never truly imagined it—as Lucas now did with every touch, every breath?

For a woman who now was worth millions, Meg would give up every penny for Lucas's arms to stay around her for the rest of her life….

Dear Reader,

This month, Silhouette Desire celebrates sensuality. All six steamy novels perfectly describe those unique pleasures that gratify our senses, like *seeing* the lean body of a cowboy at work, *smelling* his earthy scent, *tasting* his kiss…and *hearing* him say, "I love you."

Feast your eyes on June's MAN OF THE MONTH, the tall, dark and incredibly handsome single father of four in beloved author Barbara Boswell's *That Marriageable Man!* In bestselling author Lass Small's continuing series, THE KEEPERS OF TEXAS, a feisty lady does her best to tame a reckless cowboy and he winds up unleashing *her* wild side in *The Hard-To-Tame Texan*. And a dating service guarantees delivery of a husband-to-be in *Non-Refundable Groom* by ultrasexy writer Patty Salier.

Plus, Modean Moon unfolds the rags-to-riches story of an honorable lawman who fulfills a sudden socialite's deepest secret desire in *Overnight Heiress*. In Catherine Lanigan's *Montana Bride,* a bachelor hero introduces love and passion to a beautiful virgin. And a rugged cowboy saves a jilted lady in *The Cowboy Who Came in From the Cold* by Pamela Macaluso.

These six passionate stories are sure to leave you tingling… and anticipating next month's sensuous selections. Enjoy!

Regards,

Melissa Senate

Melissa Senate
Senior Editor
Silhouette Books

Please address questions and book requests to:
Silhouette Reader Service
U.S.: 3010 Walden Ave., P.O. Box 1325, Buffalo, NY 14269
Canadian: P.O. Box 609, Fort Erie, Ont. L2A 5X3

MODEAN
MOON
OVERNIGHT HEIRESS

SILHOUETTE *Desire*®

Published by Silhouette Books

America's Publisher of Contemporary Romance

If you purchased this book without a cover you should be aware
that this book is stolen property. It was reported as "unsold and
destroyed" to the publisher, and neither the author nor the
publisher has received any payment for this "stripped book."

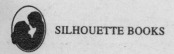

SILHOUETTE BOOKS

ISBN 0-373-76150-3

OVERNIGHT HEIRESS

Copyright © 1998 by Modean Moon

All rights reserved. Except for use in any review, the reproduction
or utilization of this work in whole or in part in any form by any
electronic, mechanical or other means, now known or hereafter
invented, including xerography, photocopying and recording, or in
any information storage or retrieval system, is forbidden without
the written permission of the editorial office, Silhouette Books,
300 East 42nd Street, New York, NY 10017 U.S.A.

All characters in this book have no existence outside the imagination of
the author and have no relation whatsoever to anyone bearing the same
name or names. They are not even distantly inspired by any individual
known or unknown to the author, and all incidents are pure invention.

This edition published by arrangement with Harlequin Books S.A.

® and TM are trademarks of Harlequin Books S.A., used under license.
Trademarks indicated with ® are registered in the United States Patent
and Trademark Office, the Canadian Trade Marks Office and in other
countries.

Printed in U.S.A.

MODEAN MOON

once believed she could do anything she wanted. Now she realizes there is not enough time in one's life to do everything. As a result, she says her writing is a means of exploring paths not taken. Currently she works as a land-title researcher, determining land or mineral ownership for clients. Modean lives in Oklahoma on a hill over-looking a small town. She shares a restored Victorian farmhouse with a six-pound dog, a twelve-pound cat, and, reportedly, a resident ghost.

One

_____

Two plainclothes policemen stood at the end of the bar.

Meg stopped just inside the door and looked warily at the two strangers, knowing they were cops without ever having seen them before. Then, with her heart beating a heavy cadence to the beat of her footsteps on the hardwood floor, she made her way through the scrubbed-clean tables and upended chairs.

They're not here for me. They can't be here for me, she told herself as she schooled her features into an expression of concerned curiosity.

"Good morning," she said pleasantly. "Is Patrick—" As she glanced around the brightly lighted room, her concern became real. "Patrick McBean is here, isn't he?"

The younger of the two men flashed a smile and just as easily flashed his ID at her. "Yes. He's in the back."

Meg let an eyebrow climb a fraction of an inch. "Is there a problem?" she asked.

The older cop, a stereotype of her worst nightmares, raked

a glance over the black tailored slacks and white pin-tucked shirt she wore on her angular body. "You a waitress here?"

"Day bartender," Meg told him, and started to pass him to go behind the bar.

"Don't touch anything."

"What?" Meg stopped in her reach for her apron.

"Not until the print crew gets here. And we're going to need your prints, too. For comparison."

Oh, hell. Oh, God. Oh, no.

The detective's eyes narrowed. "You got a problem with being printed, Miss—?"

Meg sighed. "Wilson. Meg Wilson. And yes, I have a problem in principle with workplace fingerprinting, work-place polygraph testing and random drug tests. But since my objections are based on my interpretation of constitutional rights, I don't suppose those objections will carry any weight with you, will they?"

Shut your mouth, Meg. Shut it now. This isn't the time to bait a bear. Too much is at risk.

"Isn't she something?" Patrick asked, coming in from the back room and draping his arm affectionately over Meg's shoulder.

"Night school. I swear, she can hold her own with any-body who comes in this joint. And they love it." The bar's owner squeezed her shoulder with a little more force than necessary. A warning? "Now tell these fine gentlemen you were only staying in practice, Meg, me darlin'."

Back off. Meg's silent warning to herself echoed Patrick's. *Your prints aren't on file. They can't learn anything. Don't antagonize them. Don't make them want to look past the obvious.*

Meg had a wide and generous smile. She knew: she'd had to work at it. "I'm sorry," she said, using that smile. "Wise-cracks have gotten to be such a part of the job, I sometimes think I put on the personality when I put on the rest of the uniform."

Meg turned toward her boss, but now her smile was gen-uine and concerned. "What happened this time, Patrick?"

Meg paced her minuscule living room, stopping sporadically in her marching to look out through the sliding patio door at the vibrant colors on the surviving trees in this older neighborhood—looking for peace in the panorama of changing seasons, finding none. Tulsa was big enough to get lost in, big enough to escape from, but not big enough to hide two persons from a concentrated search.

Three days had passed since the latest theft from Patrick's upscale bar and grill, three days since her fingerprints had been sent to the FBI wonderland that cops worshiped. She'd never been printed before, but...but, but, but. There were too many unknowns in this equation, and Meg was so tired—tired of running, tired of hiding—exhausted from the effort of making a home that didn't feel like they were running or hiding.

She glanced at her watch, as utilitarian as everything she wore, and grimaced. Twenty minutes; that's all she had until the neighborhood filled with the laughter and noise of home-bound school children. Twenty minutes to pace, to wrestle with her conscience, to decide. She wouldn't be able to use Patrick as a reference if she left—she'd probably never be able to contact him again.

That was what hurt: losing the friend, not the reference. But if she left without notice, would she become a suspect in this string of thefts from Patrick? Would the police look for her for that reason when they might otherwise overlook her if she stayed quietly where she was?

The doorbell squawked out half its two-note warning and crackled into silence. Meg twisted her watch face into view.

Twenty minutes. Damn it! She needed that time to pull her racing thoughts together, to drag her crumbling composure around her. Later she'd have time for the visit with her elderly neighbor, Mrs. Henson, that the woman was beginning to expect, but not now. Please, not now.

Two men stood on Meg's tiny doorstep. They were dressed in conservatively styled, tailored and colored suits. *FBI.* Her mind had no trouble making that connection.

"Good afternoon, Miss Wilson," one said as both men produced identification.

"Good afternoon," Meg said through a suddenly and agonizingly dry throat. Yes. FBI. And it wasn't an accident. They weren't just canvasing the neighborhood. They knew her name.

"What... Is something wrong?"

One of them smiled, and she was sure it had to be a violation of at least one rule. "No, ma'am. But we'd like for you to come to our office with us."

"Am I—am I under arrest for something?" FBI. Had he filed kidnapping charges? No. Even he wouldn't do that. *Of course he would!*

"Oh, no, Miss Wilson. It's just a problem that was brought out when you were fingerprinted last week. It won't take long. You should be home—within an hour."

With the deed to the Brooklyn Bridge, Meg thought. She opened the door wide and stepped back. "I need to get my purse," she said. *And I need thirty seconds alone in the bathroom. Please, please don't come in.*

Lucas Lambert was waiting in the interrogation room when the woman was brought in. He'd argued that interrogation wouldn't be necessary, but the Feds seemed to think it would be. The woman was tall, at least five-ten, he suspected, even in the flat-heeled shoes she wore, angular—almost gaunt—with her dark hair cropped in a utilitarian, no-care style, and dark eyes that would have had him questioning her relationship to Edward Carlton even without the fingerprints.

Dark eyes that called too vividly to his mind the memory of another woman facing another roomful of unknown men, another interrogation that had a far different outcome from the one he expected here. With the constant regret that he had not been there for that woman, he forced his attention back to the woman in this room.

She was frightened, although she hid it well. She took the

seat she was told to take and looked around the small room, focusing suspicious attention on him.

Hadn't these idiots told her anything? He'd relayed Edward's message to them, the same message Edward had given him when he first voiced his own suspicions. "We were rich kids," Edward had told him. "Nothing was left to chance. We were measured and fingerprinted *and* tattooed. The fingerprints convinced me, but she might need a little extra persuasion." And then Edward had given him childhood photographs showing a birthmark and a tattoo.

Scared. She was scared out of her skull, and hiding it well enough to fool most people, but not him. He focused on her hands, long fingered and slender, held loosely in her lap but trembling with the tension of not clenching them.

She visibly relaxed her hands, then lifted her chin in a cocky, do-or-die attitude. "Don't you think it's time for someone to tell me why I'm here?"

The two federal agents remained silent. Lucas stepped forward. They might not approve of his tactics later, but they had passed the ball to him. "Miss Wilson," he said. "My name is Lucas Lambert. I'm sheriff of Avalon, New Mexico."

"I don't believe I've ever been in your jurisdiction, Sheriff."

He met her cautious smile with one of his own. "That isn't surprising. Few have. But we have a new citizen of Avalon, a man who has become a good friend of mine. I'm here on his behalf."

He saw the tension return to her hands. Curious. And still more curious.

"His name is Edward Carlton."

Lucas saw no recognition in her eyes but he did note that once again her tension relaxed. "Actually, it's Edward William Renberg Carlton IV."

He watched as she fought back a smile, the same response he had once made to the pomposity of Edward's name.

"I hope he's a big man," she said.

"He is. Six-two, but lean. Dark hair. Dark eyes."

He watched the confusion in her eyes for only two heart-beats. "Edward is thirty-five now," he told her. "Twenty-five years ago his father, his mother and his younger sister went on an outing without him. Edward was left at home for some infraction—a punishment that saved his life.

"The family was kidnapped. A ransom note was received but as too often happens, somehow, someone slipped up. The bodies of Edward's mother and father were found a month later. Nothing was heard from or about his sister Megan until last week when her fingerprints turned up in a routine screening in a burglary investigation."

The tension whooshed out of her. She sank back in the chair, eyes wide, mouth open in a question she couldn't seem to speak. Lucas passed an envelope containing two pictures across the table to her. Numbly she opened the envelope and examined the pictures Edward had provided.

"And I—oh. Oh, my." She closed her eyes and turned the photographs facedown on the table, sitting silently for several seconds before she again looked up at him. For only a moment her eyes pleaded with him for—for what?—for information on who she had been, where she had lived, and what had happened to the brother she never knew?—before they shuttered.

"I suppose you want me to go with a matron or someone to prove I have those marks?"

Lucas shook his head. "No. Those photographs are for your assurance only. I'm sure there will be all sorts of for-malities to go through later, but we're satisfied with the fin-gerprints. And with your appearance. Would you like to see a picture of your brother, Miss Wilson?"

She didn't answer. Lucas didn't suppose that was too sur-prising considering the circumstances. The FBI report stated she worked as a day bartender in a popular downtown res-taurant and lived in a neighborhood that was still safe but was well past its prime. She was wearing what had to be her uniform. Everything about her was squeaky clean but func-tional; there were no frills in Meg Wilson's—Carlton's—life. That would change. That would definitely change.

Lucas considered the other photographs he had brought with him and handed her one of Edward and his new wife Jennie taken in the back garden of their home in Avalon.

Meg studied the photo, and for a moment Lucas saw what he could only describe as wistfulness play across her expression. Then her chin jutted and a cocky smile lifted her lips. "He seems to have survived his ordeal fairly well."

What the hell was she so mad about? Because Lucas was sure that anger was what he saw in her—maybe unacknowledged, maybe even unwanted, but anger just the same.

"Perhaps you'd like this one better," he said, fighting his own anger at her response. He handed her a studio portrait of Edward taken a year before, showing him as an ambitious, successful, driven—empty—man before Jennie had healed him.

Meg studied the portrait. For a moment her features, a feminine version of Edward's—a stunningly beautiful feminine version of Edward's, Lucas suddenly realized—became as bleak as those of the man he had first met only months before.

"So," she said. "What's my name?" She dropped the photo onto the table in front of her. "Who am I?"

Her name was Megan Elizabeth Carlton, and she would be twenty-nine years old in three months. Twenty-nine. It wasn't often a woman got to celebrate her twenty-ninth and her thirtieth birthdays twice. Meg's lips twisted against bitter anger. That explained so much. What was slow or backward or just plain stupid for a six-year-old—and she had been called all of those—or immature for a twelve- or an eighteen-year-old, was pretty remarkable for someone more than a year and a half younger.

No wonder she hadn't been able to cope with Blake. She hadn't been old enough to marry him when she'd divorced him.

Her parents—her adoptive parents—had some serious questions to answer. To her, and to the FBI. Had they known how young she truly was? Or had the lie about her age started before she was brought to them? It mattered; yes, knowing the answer to that question mattered. But letting them know who she was and where she was meant the possibility of Blake finding out, too. And she wasn't ready for that yet.

Not yet.

Meg schooled her features to reveal none of her thoughts. Lambert's attention seemed to be focused on the traffic as he guided his rental car back to her apartment, but more than once she had caught him studying her with more perception than normal suspicion. She ought to be terrified of him, being locked in the confines of this less-than-spacious rental car. He was dark, vaguely Native American, vaguely Arabic in appearance, and massive, but for some reason he wasn't threatening in the way she had come to expect from her past history with cops. He didn't look like a cop—maybe that was the difference.

And then Meg realized that he did. But he looked like a cop who had spent his life deflecting assaults and abuses away from those who couldn't defend themselves and taking them on himself if necessary. Or a gladiator, maybe. With battle scars that not even the civilized veneer of expensive tailoring could hide.

"Have you about got it figured out?"

Lambert's voice was still a surprise. His gravelly accent bore traces of the South—aristocracy, not Appalachia—and he spoke softly as though he had spent years allowing nothing more obvious than a whisper. And once again, his perception intimidated her.

"What?"

"Whatever it was that threw you into that poor, pitiful female, 'I'm going to faint' routine. Have you ever fainted in your life?"

Meg let out a deep breath and shook her head. "Turn left at the next light."

"Who are you hiding from?"

Not a cop? This man was wasted on some hick town. "Turn left again and find a place about midblock to park."

Lucas pulled the car to the curb and killed the engine, but when Meg reached for the door handle, he stopped her with a firm hand on her arm and an equally firm shake of his head.

"I know this is a shock to you," he said. "I know there are going to be all sorts of changes in your life—changes that no one at this time can even imagine. But I also have to know if I'm taking trouble back to Avalon. If I'm taking more trouble back to Edward and Jennie. They don't need it.

"You were scared spitless when they brought you into the interrogation room, you refused to go to Edward's house until you learned about the publicity that's sure to find you if you don't, and you faked a faint so you wouldn't have to give any details of your life beyond the past six months. That spells hiding to me, lady, and it's time I had some answers."

Meg sank back against the seat. Maybe Lambert wasn't her friend, but at least he wasn't her enemy. It wasn't as though she could keep this secret forever, anyway.

"Wrong. I faked the faint to keep from talking *and* to get out of there. And I promise you all the answers you need, but first I have to go in that house."

Lucas held her arm for perhaps a second longer. Then, with a nod, he released her. Meg scrambled from the car, had her key in her hand by the time she reached her door and went directly to the bedroom. The little stash of cash and credit cards on the top shelf of her closet was gone. She didn't have to check for the rest; she knew it would have been taken, too.

Meg sagged against the door frame, allowing herself a moment's weakness, and then went to find Lambert.

He had followed her into the house but had stopped at the open door to the bathroom. The medicine cabinet door stood at an angle, and the message she had scrawled on it was obvious even though she had only had cold cream to use.

"'B'?" he asked.

"As in Plan B," Meg told him. "Everyone talks about

one. We actually had one. And an A and even a C. Today
had all the earmarks of a B day.''

"Answers, Meg."

She nodded, swallowed once and squared her shoulders.
"It's been a long time since I've been able to trust anyone,
Lambert. It doesn't come easily." She took a towel from the
hamper and began wiping the cold cream from the mirror.

Lucas stilled her motions, took the towel from her and
rested both hands on her shoulders. "Answers," he said in
his whispery voice.

For a moment Meg accepted the comfort of this man's
hands on her shoulders. He was strong enough for her to
lean against if she but would, and for that moment she
wanted very much to do just that, to let someone else fend
off the fears and frustrations that had become her life. But
she suspected that too many people had already done that to
Lucas Lambert; she wouldn't add unnecessarily to the bur-
dens he carried. And besides, she remembered with a small
start of surprise, he was a cop.

She stepped back, drawing her strength around her. "Your
friend Edward isn't just regaining his long-lost sister today,"
she said. "He's getting a little more family than that."

"Meg—"

"Can I tell you the rest of it later?" she asked. "Right
now we have to stop my son before he gets on a plane to
Florida."

Danny looked like her. Too thin, too intense, too competent in his escape plans to be a novice at Plan B or any other
plan, and too world-weary to be the twelve Meg had told
him.

Now the boy was asleep, curled up in a seat by a window
of the Carlton executive jet—the aftereffects of too much
adrenaline in too short a time. Lucas knew the symptoms
well.

What he didn't know was why these two were running,
or how they had become so accomplished at it.

Megan had taken one quick, startled breath when she'd

seen the interior of Edward's private jet. Lucas thought that before that point the fact of Edward's wealth hadn't really penetrated through her shock at finding herself with family. She had sunk silently into one of the oversize chairs grouped for conversation at the front of the cabin. Now she looked up, catching Lucas in his study of the sleeping boy. He watched as the silent battle she waged with herself played through her expressive eyes, watched as she imperceptibly squared her shoulders and prepared herself physically for battle.

"How many times am I going to have to tell this story, Sheriff?" Meg finally said.

Lucas shook his head. "I don't know. There is no statute of limitations on murder. And the Bureau is going to want to drag every possible bit of memory it can from you. Edward won't push you, but he's going to want to know what happened to you. And it seems to me that there are some things I will have to know, in order to protect you from whatever it is that has you running."

Meg nodded. "Fair enough. But why don't you make a note of the things you think are going to be important to the—to the past—and have them typed into a statement, or something, that I can sign and not have to go through this again?"

"We can try that," Lucas told her. *We can damn well try,* he vowed. This woman looked like she had been through hell and was on the verge of being thrust back into it.

But this time he would make sure that nothing—*nothing*—got past him to harm her. It was a promise he now knew he had made the moment he had looked into her eyes and seen again the vivid reminder of the debt that was the only hope of redemption for his misbegotten life.

He could help this woman.

She was as fragile as his wife, Alicia, had been in those last few months after he'd come back to her, as fragile as Jennie had been when she first came to Avalon, although he suspected Meg would never admit to fragility—to weakness of any kind.

He could give her the security and protection she needed to discover who she was and who she could become. Her son would have the chance to be a child again, and in a few months, when she left, when she no longer needed him, he could deal with that, too.

Could he?

Giving was hard. Much harder than he'd ever dreamed when he'd promised that if he lived, he would learn to give. Give, rather than take. Give, rather than accept as somehow due.

Give, because if he never got anything else in return, he had already received more than he could ever give back.

But he suspected that Megan Elizabeth Carlton presented more of a challenge to his sanity and his soul than he had faced since he'd made that promise. Could he give to her and her son Danny without asking anything in return from them? Would he be able to let them leave—let her leave—without relinquishing a vital part of the soul he was trying so hard to redeem?

And even if he couldn't, did he any longer have a choice?

TWO

Meg leaned back in the luxuriously upholstered chair and closed her eyes, wondering where to start in telling the convoluted but not terribly interesting story of her life.

For a moment her senses became finely attuned to her surroundings—the hushed drone of the powerful engine, the fine fabric of the upholstery, the deep pile of the carpet, the unmistakable aroma of "new" and "clean."

Everything about the jet's passenger compartment was designed to cushion and protect its occupants, much as the Carlton wealth would cushion and protect.

Meg felt a wave of anger as uncontrollable and as unwanted as the one she had felt when she first saw a picture of the man they told her was her brother—laughing, carefree, with his arm around his wife in the security of their own home.

Secure, happy, protected—while she and Danny ran from city to city, from furnished apartment to hotel room, from one minimum-wage job to the next. She pushed those thoughts away, recognizing her rare flash of jealousy as both unreasonable and unwarranted. She had done nothing to earn this wealth. And she and Danny had always had each other.

Still, with the Carlton wealth behind her, she might not have had to hide so desperately from Blake...wouldn't have been able to—

Enough!

Recognizing that her random thoughts were merely postponing the inevitable, Meg opened her eyes to find Lucas Lambert studying her from the adjacent chair.

"Are you all right now?" he asked.

Meg saw concern in Lambert's gray eyes, concern and secrets she couldn't begin to guess. But his secrets weren't under examination now; hers were.

"Are you going to take notes?"

Lambert gestured toward the table between them, and Meg noticed controls and some sort of built-in equipment.

"I can take notes, or we can tape what you tell me. It's your decision."

Meg sighed. "Please take notes. I don't think I'm going to say anything earthshaking, but I—I've never been comfortable with the idea of not knowing who is going to be listening."

Lambert nodded and took a small notebook and what appeared to be a gold pen from an inside jacket pocket.

"Where do I start?"

"Meg, this isn't an inquisition, but would it be easier if I asked you some questions?"

"No. No, I wasn't thinking. Of course I know what you need me to tell you.

"I grew up in Simonville. That's a small town about forty-five miles east of Sacramento. I was adopted—I think I always knew that—at least from the time I started school onward.

"My adoptive parents were—are—James and Audrey Stemple. They called me Margaret Ann—maybe I was able to cling to the name Meg—I don't know. He was a judge. She is the daughter of a doctor. Other members of the family told me that they had wanted a child for years. The story was that I was the daughter of a distant niece, although I knew that wasn't true, but I don't know how I knew. They may have told me."

Meg paused, collecting her memories.

"They—Audrey especially—told me a lot of things when they were angry," she added, unable to keep her remembered pain from tingeing her words.

"I don't remember much of my early childhood, very little before the first grade. I had a lot of trouble in the first grade. And the second." Meg caught her hand to her mouth. "And the third."

"Discipline?" Lucas asked.

Meg heard a barely hidden thread of humor in his voice. Well he might ask, she thought, considering the chase she had taken him on today. And she wished now that her problems had been discipline; Lucas Lambert could have understood that, perhaps even have appreciated it. And for some inexplicable reason, his good opinion had become important to her.

"No," she said, plunging onward. Good opinion, bad opinion or no opinion, she had to get this story told and behind her. "Academic. I almost failed first grade, and all through the elementary grades I had to fight to barely keep up with the class."

"Now *that* I find difficult to believe."

"So did James and Audrey. Audrey especially. She explained to me time after time how I was going to have to do better, that as their daughter I had an image to uphold and that they had gone to great lengths to give me the advantages of their home, their name…"

"You know there are a number of valid reasons why an obviously bright child doesn't learn in school."

She sighed and rewarded him with a smile that was genuine and free of any artifice.

"Thank you for that. And yes, now I do know. And now—today, in fact—I can at last begin to accept that I gave them no reason to be disappointed in me." She had to ask. She had to hear again the words that freed her from a cruel and untrue childhood label—dumb, stupid, slow; Audrey had screamed all of those at her—but she was afraid that somehow she had heard Lucas wrong, had misunderstood, had wanted so badly to believe that she'd manufactured an excuse. "Tell me again the date of my birthday."

"January 20?" Lucas said, but she heard the unspoken question in his voice.

"And Meg Carlton will be twenty-nine?"

"Yes."

Meg felt moisture glittering in her eyes. She hadn't misheard; she hadn't misunderstood. "Write this down, Sheriff. Margaret Ann Stemple's birth certificate swears that five months ago she passed her thirtieth birthday."

Lambert was silent, so silent that Meg looked up at him. He was watching her, quietly, intently, while running his gold pen through his fingers. "It would seem to me," he said finally, "that James and Audrey have a great deal to answer for—the 'great lengths' they went to to obtain someone else's child, and why they so obviously failed to cherish that child once they had her."

Cherish. Yes. That was precisely the right word for how Meg loved her own son. But how strange to hear that kind of comment come with such ease from someone who looked as though he had never been cherished, either. How strange it was that this stern and unsmiling man, this man who had known her only superficially and only for a few hours, should know instinctively what had been missing from her life.

"How are they with Danny?"

Caught in her thoughts, Meg almost didn't hear the question, and then she wished she hadn't. "They aren't," she said abruptly, because now Lambert had come to the hard questions. "They've never seen Danny."

She had met Blake Wilson when she was a senior in high school. She'd been tall even then, all arms and legs and knees and elbows and so hungry for affection that she had believed everything Blake told her, everything he promised.

"They didn't approve of Blake, Danny's father," she told

Lambert. "When we—decided to marry, they told me not to bother to come back to them when the marriage failed. When the marriage did fail, I—I believed what they had told me."

"And the boy's father?"

"Is the reason we're running."

Lambert had gone still, holding his pen between his fingers, not moving.

"He's abusive," Meg said, condensing years of pain into those two words. "The last time he found us, two years ago, he broke Danny's arm."

A pencil would have snapped under the pressure. "Did the bastard go to jail?" Lambert asked with deadly quiet.

And now for the moment of truth. Meg glanced around the luxuriously appointed jet. She was only beginning to suspect the power and wealth of the Carlton family—enough power and wealth that Lucas Lambert, the sheriff, would continue to protect her and her son, but would Lucas Lambert, the man, believe her?

"No."

Lambert placed his notebook on the table between them and aligned the gold pen beside it. "Why not?"

Meg fisted her hands to keep from reaching for his pen, for his hand—to touch him or any part of him in some—any—way. Where were all these unfamiliar urgings coming from?

"We were in Denver," she told him, calmly, dispassionately. She was making a report as once before she had made a related report. "A nice young patrol officer came to the emergency room. I filed a complaint. By then Blake had come to the hospital, too. He can be…very convincing. He showed the nice young officer his own police commission—he's a detective captain in Simonville—swapped a few stories about his father, the chief of police, and his grandfather in the 'good old days' of the department, threw in a blatant fabrication about a contested custody suit and convinced everyone there except one doctor that I was a vindictive, hysterical ex-wife."

"This—this man is still a police officer?" Lambert asked, and Meg heard not one clue to his thoughts or his feelings.

"Yes. At least I think he still is. He left once a few years ago to do something he thought more exciting—DEA, I think—but he went back to Simonville."

"You're divorced?"

"Yes. Yes, of course."

"And you have custody of Danny?"

"Yes."

"Good. That simplifies things. Not that it really matters. If you weren't, or didn't, a battery of lawyers would go to work tomorrow. Will anyway, if you want them to. Are you vindictive, Meg? Do you want his job? His hide? A pound or two of flesh?"

Did she? If she were truly honest, she'd have to admit that at one time she had wanted Blake to suffer for the pain he had caused Danny and for the unsettled and too-frequently disrupted life they were forced to lead. Then her fantasies had been just that—dark-of-the-night fantasies with no hope of ever being fulfilled. Now? Now she could no more ask than she could have when she was still Meg Wilson, struggling single mother.

She shook her head. "No," she said. "No. I just want him to leave us alone."

"You don't need the Carlton legal staff for that, Meg," Lucas told her with promise in every softly spoken word. "Just me. And I swear to you, as long as I'm around, he'll have to go through me before he ever lays a hand on either you or Danny again."

Avalon, New Mexico, was as much a surprise to Meg as its soft-spoken sheriff had been. But in a day when her world had been literally turned around, she didn't suppose she should be surprised by geography, no matter how unexpected it was.

The jet landed at a small, but obviously modern, airport in what seemed to her to be little more than a wide clearing in the forested mountains. From the plane she'd seen a white-spired, picture-postcard village a little further up the mountain.

Meg awakened Danny, who scrambled upright in his window seat and strapped himself in for the landing. He was no more surprised than she by the terrain below them—the former-ocean-bed desert stretching in one direction and the awesome pine-covered mountains in the other—he just didn't hide his surprise as well as she.

And he didn't manage to hide his involuntary shrinking away when Lucas reached to help him into the top-of-the-line Land Rover that waited for them at a terminal straight out of an art deco design book.

Meg saw Lucas's mouth flatten into a narrow, unsmiling line, but he unobtrusively stepped back, giving Danny the space he needed without calling attention to that need. He gave Meg the same space, not touching her, as he held the door for the passenger-side front seat.

Almost in the center of town, he turned into the graveled driveway of a walled estate that wound its way through an arborist's sampler of trees and shrubs to a large, stone and timbered house. The house should have been imposing because of its size, but instead Meg found it surprisingly welcoming.

Meg sat still while Lucas rounded the Land Rover and opened the door for her; she'd lost the duel of the doors twice in Tulsa and knew that he would insist on this courtly gesture no matter whether she was seventeen or seventy. Danny remained in his seat, and she suspected it was because he was temporarily intimidated by his surroundings. She'd explained to him what Lambert had told her as best she could when they had retrieved him from the Tulsa airport, but she knew he was having as much trouble as she was—maybe more—understanding the changes in their lives.

She smelled the pleasant aroma of wood smoke from a fireplace chimney and felt the promise of a light chill in the air of approaching night, a chill that the wealth and comfort of the house they faced would cushion.

Lucas Lambert held his hand out to her to help her from

the vehicle. She glanced at it, at the strength evident in its wide palm and long, blunt fingers, and hesitated. She never asked for help—*never*—but this man insisted on giving it to her. Why? What was there about her, or him, that made him do so? And what was there about her, or him, that made her want to take that help? Not just in alighting from a car, but in facing what waited for her inside that huge stone house, in facing what waited for her when Blake found out who and where she was?

She lifted her chin and placed her hand in his, taking his help as she stepped from the vehicle and onto the winter green grass bordering the drive.

For a moment his hand closed over hers, wrapping it in a promise of safety and caring and concern that she had no memory of ever knowing, wrapping it in a promise of more, much more. Stunned, she looked up, surprising for no more than a second a look in his eyes that spoke of hunger and longing and a loneliness as great as she had known for most of her life. And then it was gone, replaced by a professional, or perhaps a distant-relation, friendliness.

She drew in a not-quite-steady breath and gave him a shaky smile before turning toward her son. "Come on, Danny," she said softly. "Let's go meet this new family of ours."

"Yeah," he mumbled. "It's for sure they've got to be better than the old one."

Meg let the uncharacteristic bitterness pass without comment. She had felt something similar when faced with the apparent ease of Edward Carlton's life when contrasted with hers. His studio portrait had proved her mistaken about just how sheltered and comfortable he had been. Something would prove it to Danny, too, but until it did, nothing she said would change his mind.

Double oak doors, framed by a heavily leaded, stained-glass fanlight and matching panels, guarded the entrance to the house. Before their little entourage reached the flat, protected landing, one of those doors flew open, spilling light out into the darkening night and revealing the tall, stern man of the photograph and a small, delicate young woman as light and effervescent as a butterfly.

"You brought them?" the young woman said. "Sheriff Lambert? You really brought them."

"Yes, Miss Jennie," Lucas answered, stepping to Meg's side to grasp the young woman's hands. "Now what are you doing running around like this? Aren't you supposed to be resting?"

The tall, stern man—it had to be Edward, *her brother*—dropped his hand onto the woman's—onto Jennie's— shoulder. "Yes, she is," he said. "But you know Jennie."

He looked out onto the steps, and his eyes—eyes that were achingly familiar to her from all the times she had looked into a mirror—locked with Meg's.

"Meggie?" he said. "Oh, God." His voice broke, and Meg saw a glint of moisture in his eyes. "It really is you. Meggie."

Jennie lifted a hand to grasp Edward's where it lay on her shoulder. "Of course it is," she said. But even her voice seemed strangely thick. Then, smiling, she stepped away from Edward's touch and out onto the porch. "He really wants to do this," she said to Meg, "but he's still learning that it's all right to show his emotions. Give him a little more time, though, and you'll be able to see the love that's in him, too." Then she wrapped her arms around Meg and hugged her tightly. "We're so glad we found you. Edward's missed you forever."

With one last welcoming hug, Jennie stepped back and looked toward the young boy standing slightly behind Meg, a boy who, in spite of his youth, was almost as tall as she. "And you're Danny. Lucas told us about you when he called from Tulsa, but no one would ever have had to tell me who you are. You're going to look just like your Uncle Edward."

Danny shrugged and nodded, clearly unsure of his welcome or how he should act toward this strange woman, in spite of her words. Meg took a comforting step closer to him.

"I suppose you're too big to admit wanting a hug," Jennie said to the boy. When Danny shrugged and nodded again,

Jennie smiled. "Too bad," she said as she stepped up to him and wrapped him in an embrace. "Everybody needs hugs."

Danny didn't immediately surrender to the embrace, but he didn't struggle, either. Meg caught him looking at her in questioning wonder and gave him a shrug of her own.

"And everybody needs to come into the house and get out of the night air," Edward said, stepping back but holding out his hand toward Jennie.

"Yes, Miss Jennie," Lambert added, looking pointedly at her. "They do."

Jennie laughed and turned, wrapping one arm over Danny's shoulder and the other around Meg's waist. "Then by all means, let's *everybody* go inside."

Only then did Meg notice the lines of pain on the young woman's face. Only then did she hear the strain in her voice. *Curious,* she thought, as she let herself and her son be led into the house, down a long, wide hall with hardwood floors and Oriental rugs. Fine English side tables and crystal wall sconces lined the walls on the way to what must have been considered a small room in that house, but which was welcoming and comfortably furnished, with a cheery wood fire burning in the cozy fireplace.

There, Edward firmly but gently led Jennie to a wing chair and stood in front of her until she grinned at him and settled herself in the chair. Then, as though not really sure of the etiquette—and who could be, Meg wondered—he gestured toward the other chairs in the grouping. "Please," he said. "Make yourself comfortable. I—" He broke off with a short laugh. "I really don't know what to say next. And I suppose you are as much in the dark as I am."

He turned fully toward her. He was tall. As tall as Lucas Lambert who stood beside him, although he was leaner and didn't have the look of being battle scarred that Lambert wore so unconsciously. And it was more than just his eyes that were familiar to her from her time at the mirror.

"Meggie," he said again, and his voice made her name a prayer. "I knew—I knew it had to be you when your prints matched," he told her. "And Lucas told us how much—how much you bore the family resemblance. But, God!..."

Jennie reached for his hand and grasped it.

Edward straightened and glanced toward Lambert. "You'll stay for dinner?" he asked.

Lucas shook his head, and Meg felt an unreasonable sense of betrayal at being abandoned by him. "Sorry," he said. "I've got work stacked up at the office and more coming as a result of today." He turned toward Jennie. "You take care of yourself, now," he said softly.

He looked again at Edward. "The news shouldn't break for a few days, but if you need me, you know to call."

He turned toward Danny. "You're a fine young man," he said, and Megan heard in his words a goodbye, to Danny and to her. "It's been a pleasure meeting you."

And then he turned toward her. "And—and it's been a pleasure meeting you, too, Meg. If you need anything..."

Meg shook her head, stopping his polite offer. "Thank you, Sheriff Lambert," she said. So, it was to be Lucas Lambert, the sheriff, with whom she dealt in the future, and not Lucas Lambert, the man. For a while she had wondered. For a while she had almost let herself hope. "You've been more than kind. I appreciate all you've done for us."

Tully Wilbanks, his first deputy, was still on duty when Lucas arrived at headquarters. He summoned Tully back to his office and waited until the deputy shut the door. Then he shrugged out of his suit jacket and draped it across his chair. Stretching once, he sighed and leaned against the desk.

"Tough trip?" Tully asked.

Lucas shook his head. "Surprising, but not strenuous."

"Was she?"

Was she Megan Carlton and not an impostor? It was amazing how many normally intelligent people thought someone who didn't claim to be anyone other than a single mother and daytime bartender could be scheming to be Megan Carlton. Even he had, he remembered. At first. "She is."

''Wow. I guess now we're going to have reporters and feds crawling all over the place.''

''Reporters, maybe,'' Lucas admitted. ''But not too many feds. At least not for a while.''

''Okay,'' Tully said. ''We can handle the press. We've still got the plans we worked out when that British rock star came to visit his cousin.''

Plan B. Everyone talks about one. We actually had one. And an A and even a C.

''Tully?''

''Yeah, Lucas?''

''We may be getting a call from a Blake Wilson. He's a detective with the Simonville, California, PD, although he may claim some previous DEA connection. He'll be asking for professional consideration, and he may claim he has visitation rights with his son. He doesn't get either.''

Tully's left eyebrow went up a quarter of an inch, but he made no comment, only nodded his understanding.

''If he shows up,'' Lucas went on, ''I'm to be notified the moment he sets foot in this jurisdiction, and he's not to be allowed anywhere near Meg Carlton or her son without an escort. Will you make that clear to the department?''

Again Tully nodded.

''And will you see if you can find a picture of him, probably from the DEA, without letting him know?''

''Is he dangerous?''

Lucas considered that for a moment. ''He's a cop,'' he said finally, ''so he will be armed. He's a cop,'' he said, letting his distaste show, ''who broke his ten-year-old son's arm.''

After Tully left, Lucas leaned back in his leather chair, toed open a bottom desk drawer and propped his feet on the rim. Meg Wilson—Meg *Carlton*—had been quite a surprise for him. And he was pretty sure he had been a surprise for her—over and above the obvious stunning news of the day.

He'd felt the moment she became aware of him and of the attraction he'd felt for her. He let a rueful smile twist his face at the memory of that one brief moment, standing in front of her brother's home with her son watching as he helped her from the car: one brief moment that had no time to go anywhere before he surrendered her to her new brother and to her new life.

What on earth had made him think this woman needed him? Meg Wilson might have. But Meg Carlton? Not too likely. At least, not after the ordeal of the next few weeks had passed.

But until then, she did.

Oh, yes. Until then, she definitely did.

And did he need her? He suspected that he did. He suspected—hell, he knew, damn it!—that sometime between watching her being led into the interrogation room and helping her from the car in her brother's driveway, he had grown to need the surprising, gentle, stubborn, competent and insecure woman that Meg Carlton had become.

His chair was too well constructed and maintained to squeak when he pushed out of it, but his desk drawer closed with a satisfying slam.

He *couldn't* need her. He couldn't take from another person. Not again. Not ever. And he was afraid that if he ever admitted to needing Meg Carlton he'd want to take, have to take, and it wouldn't matter then how much he had to give, because it would never be enough.

He ran an impatient hand through his hair and then grasped the back of his neck, working his head back and forth in an attempt to release some of his tension.

Enough! he told himself. He had more to do than wallow in what he couldn't or wouldn't take.

He had responsibilities.

Shaking his head, he reached for his telephone and punched out the numbers.

"Lambert residence," answered the sweet, young-girl's voice on the other end of the line.

"Hi, kiddo."

"Pops! Are you home? Did you bring Avalon's Anastasia with you?"

Lucas surrendered to a grin. At fourteen, Jamie was only two years older than Danny, but a world apart in openness from the quiet, solemn boy, and a world apart in spontaneity from the daughter he had finally tracked down seven years ago. Russian history was her latest love. How like her to compare Meg Carlton's return with the tragic life of the youngest daughter of Czar Nicholas.

"I did," he said.

"And is she?" Jamie asked. "Really?"

"Really," he told her. "Wait till you see her. There's no way she's not Edward's sister."

"Hot da—oops!"

Lucas chuckled. "Oops is right, kiddo. You won't like the taste of soap messing up your pizza."

"You mean I don't have to force feed us broccoli tonight after all?"

Lucas shook his head. Jamie loved broccoli. But she loved pizza more. "Not tonight," he told her. "Tonight I have a craving to take my best girl out for a special meal and a night on the town."

After he hung up, he shrugged into his suit jacket and looked around the office.

It was a good office. A stable, dependable workplace after a lifetime of strife. And if Jamie was his best girl, that was his choice, too. A choice he had willingly made. A choice he could live with, as he could live with the peace of Avalon, as he could live with doing what he had to do to ease the way of others, as he could live without...without the temptation that for a moment Meg Carlton so unconsciously had offered.

He couldn't need her, he told himself again. He wouldn't need her. But somehow his vows seemed pathetically lacking in force.

Three

Meg stretched and twisted, trying to get comfortable in the wide bed. She suspected she wouldn't, no matter how many times she pounded the down-filled pillows. No matter how many times she told herself that Danny was sleeping peacefully in the equally luxurious room adjoining hers. No matter how many times she realized she was living her little-girl fantasy: the king and queen had come for her—had told her, "You belong with us, my dear. We're taking you home to live in the castle," and had whisked her away from the unhappiness of life with James and Audrey, of life with Blake.

And they'd whisked her away from the insecurity of knowing that if anything happened to her, her son would be alone, unprotected and unloved. Now Danny would never be left alone. Edward would love him, and Jennie; she knew that from the few hours she had spent with them. And Lucas would protect him.

Meg slid her hand over the smooth sheet she lay on. It wasn't actually linen—she was fairly sure of that—but a cotton so luxurious that the sheets on this bed alone had to have

cost as much as the entire contents of her bedroom in Tulsa.
And across the room, in the alcove of a sitting room, the
glow from a fire in the tiny marble fireplace danced over the
pattern of an Oriental rug. Sheer luxury. Opulence in excel-
lent taste.

So why was her mind spinning, refusing to let her sleep?
Wasn't her life going to be wonderful from here on out?
After all, the glass slipper had fit.

No. That was the wrong fairy tale.

And in spite of all the times she'd wished as a child for
the king and queen to come and get her, in spite of the
pictures and videotapes of converted home movies Edward
had shown her that evening, in spite of the memories her
brother—*her brother*—had shared with her, she didn't feel
like the princess. She was just Meg Wilson, Danny's mother
and Patrick's bartender. Tomorrow she would miss an entire
shift at Patrick's. Tonight Danny had missed his woodcarv-
ers' club meeting, and she had missed a class in contract
law. That was going to be important when everyone here
discovered she was really an impostor.

Wrong. Wrong, wrong, wrong. She wasn't an impostor.
This was her life now, and no matter how strange, how *alien*
it seemed to her, she had better get used to it.

A brother. Oh, Lord, she had a brother. A family. A decent
family—she would have been drawn to Edward and Jennie
even if they hadn't been—been *hers*. And friends. She could
have friends now. Friends she wouldn't have to leave without
a word, if—when—Blake found them.

And when Blake found them this time, Lucas would be
there with her, standing between her and whatever he threatened.

Lucas.

Meg turned again, and this time her shoulder found the
spot in the feather bed that had eluded her all night, her cheek
nestled against the pillow and the tension that had clenched
her shoulders eased from her as she felt, at last, the peace of
sleep wrapping itself around her.

"Gee, Ma, you goin' to sleep all day?"

Ma? Meg raised one eyelid and glanced across the oversize pillow she had hugged to her as she slept. A dream floated back into her subconscious as she focused on Danny standing at the side of the bed. Since when did her son call her Ma? She squinted at him through sleepy eyes. Since when did her son look like an escapee from a Dumpster?

"Didn't I throw that T-shirt in the rag bin this fall?"

Danny looked down at his shirt and grinned. "Yeah, but I figured, what the heck? They're probably expecting the Beverly Hillbillies. Why not give them what they want?"

Meg closed her eyes, but all thought of sleep had fled with Danny's words. Sighing, she unwound her arms from the pillow and scooted up against the headboard, taking the sheet with her. "He's my brother, Danny. Do you have any idea what this means to me?"

"Yeah," her son told her. "It means that after today you get to sleep in silk instead of that reject from the thrift store."

She would have liked to wait until she was more awake and more sure of her own emotions before having this conversation, but it looked as if the time for waiting had fled with the last of her elusive dream.

"Are you angry with me, Danny?"

"You? No. Why?"

"Then maybe you're angry with Edward and Jenny. You do understand that they didn't know about us until the day before we found out about them, don't you? They came for us right away."

"They came for you. No. They *sent* for you. They sent a *cop* for you. I just got dragged along because—"

"Because I'd cut off my arm before I'd leave you behind?"

At that Danny ducked his head. "Yeah," he mumbled.

"And of course they've been really mean to you since you got here," Meg continued in a companionable tone. "Made you sleep in the basement, fed you gruel and water for supper last night—"

At the mention of gruel, her stomach gave an audible complaint. She looked away from Danny's answering grin and saw the delicate, ornate clock on the nearby desk. "Ten o'clock? I slept until ten o'clock? Good grief. Breakfast? Are you starved?"

"Nah. I ate hours ago. There was some old lady in the kitchen when I found it. She was cryin' when I got there, but she fixed me pancakes. I don't think you're going to get food though, not unless you cook it yourself. There's something really weird going on in this house, people going and coming, an old guy that looks like the actor that played Santa in *Miracle on 34th Street* and some sort of a preacher with one of those tight white collars up to here. And, oh yeah, the sheriff's back. Do you suppose they're going to kick us out?"

Meg shook her head. Danny's insecurity was even worse than her own, probably with good reason. She'd tried. Oh, how she had tried. Apparently her efforts so far hadn't been enough, but that didn't mean she could give up. "Edward and Jennie are family."

"Yeah. Well, so was Dad. And so were all those grandparents I've never even seen."

Now Meg was the one to duck her head. "Yeah." She chuffed out a sigh and studied her son. He was so young and so cynical, and right now, even though he'd never admit it, so scared. And so was she. "But you're right about one thing," she told him. "I suspect that we're at least part of the reason those people are here this morning. Us and the trouble that's going to come down on our heads when the press gets hold of this story."

She slid her long legs in the almost-long-enough nightgown over the side of the bed and quirked a grin at Danny. "Give me a hug so I'll have the strength to face what the day has in store, and then scram and let me get dressed so I can go face it.

"And, Danny," she said when he just stood there, "I don't think we're going anywhere, but just remember, if we do, you and me kid, we go together. Got that?"

Meg found Lucas and Edward in serious conversation in the same small sitting room they had used the night before. Edward looked up, stricken, when she entered the room.

"Meggie…"

"What's wrong?"

"Do you and Danny have passports?"

Passports? Why would they need passports? Concerned, she shook her head.

"No. Of course not," her brother said. "Or we would have found you much sooner. Lucas?"

Hearing the thread of panic in her brother's voice sparked an answering one in Meg. "What's wrong?" she repeated.

"It's Jennie. She needs surgery. We'd hoped to be able to avoid it—she'd seemed to improve—or at least to postpone it, especially since you've just arrived, but she had a relapse last night. Dr. Freede contacted her neurologist finally, about six this morning, and we need to take her…now."

"Someplace where I would need a passport to accompany you?"

He nodded. "Switzerland."

Meg found a chair simply by backing into it, and collapsed. What kind of wealth had she stumbled into? Jennie needed surgery so they woke up a couple of doctors in the middle of the night and scheduled a trip to the other side of the world.

"Is she— How is she?"

"In pain." Edward looked at her with his unbelievably familiar eyes. He'd told her the night before how close he'd come to losing Jennie, in a kidnap attempt. Now she knew he had never shed the fear of losing her to the effects of the serious head injuries she's suffered in that attempt. "Frightened," he said, "but trying not to let me see just how much. I wouldn't leave you if this wasn't critical."

Unbelievably familiar. But not quite real.

Meg sought out the only thing, the only person, in the room who was truly real to her. "Are you going, too?" she asked Lucas.

He gave her a grim smile. "Only as far as the airport."

"When?"

"Within the hour."

Within the hour. It was that critical, then. She forced her practical self to take over. "What can I do to help?"

Edward crossed the room and dropped his hand onto her shoulder. "Just be here when we get back, Meggie. Don't let us lose you again."

She sensed a deep pain in Edward's words, an echo of too many losses. Uneasy with the intimacy and the sharing that was so different from the isolation she had always known, Meg looked away—and found Lucas watching Edward's hand on her shoulder. Losses. She and Edward weren't the only ones to have felt them.

"You will be here?"

She dragged her attention back to Edward. "Yes." She knew he needed to hear her say the words. "Yes, of course."

Edward turned to the other man in the room. "And you'll take care of her?"

Lucas's eyes met hers. Reluctantly? Meg couldn't really be sure of anything but his words. "Yes," he said, echoing her promise. "Yes, of course."

They weren't truly alone in the house; at least Meg didn't think they were. But it seemed that way. For such a large house, Edward kept a very small staff. A very small, tired staff, who had been up most of the night while she and Danny slept. After assuring the cook that she would be all right, and sending her off for a much needed nap, Meg installed herself in the kitchen.

Here, at least, she felt at home.

The room was huge, with marvelous, if ancient, commercial fixtures. Except for the numerous sparkling windows, it reminded her of the kitchen at Patrick's and at any number of the restaurants where she had worked over the past twelve years.

Danny ambled into the kitchen and scooted himself up onto the long pine table in the center of the room. "I told you that if you wanted to eat, you'd have to fix it yourself," he said.

His moods never lasted long. Maybe if she just ignored this one it would go away. Meg doubted that, but it was worth at least one more try. "So you did, oh fearless prognosticator. Did you happen to foresee what I would be preparing?"

"Corn dogs, French fries and double-chocolate ice cream?"

"Hah!" Meg grabbed lettuce and a platter of baked chicken from the refrigerator. "Swami sees with a broken crystal ball."

Danny grinned at her, her mischievous and loving son again for at least this moment. "It was worth a try."

The rich were different, or at least lived differently, Meg thought moments later as she and Danny lunched on sandwiches made of thinly sliced chicken on a rich homemade dark rye bread with tangy mayonnaise that had never seen a processing plant and tomatoes that had ripened naturally somewhere in a warm climate.

"Still want corn dogs?" Meg asked as her son with the hollow leg built his second monster sandwich.

"Mmmph."

She interpreted that as a "no," or maybe a "later, Mom," and grinned. Danny's appetite, at least, had not changed.

"So," she asked, already knowing the answer, "have you had a chance to check out this place?"

Danny nodded. "Big," he said. "Big house. Big yard. Big fence." He set his sandwich on its plate and looked at her. "Did somebody really steal you when you were just a little kid?"

Not only had he been checking out the place, he'd obviously been spying on conversations, as well, because neither she nor Lucas had told him just exactly how Meg had gotten separated from her family. "That's what they tell me," she said.

"Gee. You must have been scared."

Meg nodded. "I expect I was."

"You don't *know?*"

She shook her head. "No, Danny, I don't remember."

"Then maybe it's a mistake, and you're not who they think?"

She reached across the table and took his wildly gesturing hand in hers. "Aside from the fact that my fingerprints match, remember that funny little birthmark I have behind my left ear?"

He nodded.

"Meg Carlton had one just like it. And Jennie was right. You do look like your Uncle Edward. A lot. Especially when he was your age."

"So we do belong here?"

She smiled at him. "Yes, Danny. I think at long last we have found a place where we really belong."

Lucas returned minutes after she had taken Danny to the only other downstairs room where she felt comfortable, the small sitting room, and had begun showing her son the photo albums Edward had left for her. Danny tensed when he saw the man standing in the doorway; Meg tensed when she saw the hummingbird of a woman who accompanied him.

"They're on their way?" Meg asked.

Lucas nodded.

"Yes," the woman said, just that, *yes,* as she stepped into the room. "This will be a pleasure. Oh, yes, Megan, you will be stunning."

"Excuse me?"

Lucas shook his head, and what might have been a smile passed over his features. Yes. Definitely a smile. But gone so quickly she almost missed it. "Let me introduce you. Meg Wilson, this is Marianna Richards. Marianna, this is Meg and her son Danny."

The woman smiled at Danny and advanced on her, a tiny, delicate firestorm of color and self-assurance. "Jewel tones," she said. "Definitely. And drama. Lots of drama. Scarves and hats and—oh, yes—more height. Two-inch heels. Maybe three."

"I beg your pardon," Meg said, looking from the woman to Lucas in confusion.

"Oh. Oh, I am sorry," Marianna said. "Edward has asked me to oversee your makeover."

Makeover. Meg felt every defensive hackle she possessed rise up in indignation. "Makeover," she said tightly. "I don't think so. If I'm not accepta—I'm perfectly happy with who I am."

"Oh, yes. Of course you are. And you should be. But when the reporters come, and they will, snapping around like a pack of ill-mannered little terriers, you are going to want to look down your lovely aristocratic nose at them and silence them. I'm just here as a friend of the family—for no other reason, I assure you—to help you be able to do that."

And to make sure I look like a Carlton, Meg thought. But of course she couldn't say that. And why shouldn't she look like someone who belonged to this wealth, she realized; she *was* a Carlton. Even though she didn't feel like one. Maybe she did need this woman's help. She looked up and caught Lucas studying her quietly from across the room, not condemning, just offering a steady, nonjudgmental acceptance of whatever she decided to do.

"And me? Are you going to try to make me over, too?" Danny asked with the same belligerence Meg had heard in his voice earlier that morning.

Marianna turned slowly toward him and raked an appraising glance from hair he had managed somehow to spike, over disreputable T-shirt and jeans, to athletic shoes that looked as though he had found a mud puddle to scrape them through.

"That's quite a fashion statement," she said. "How old are you? Twelve?" She glanced back at Lucas. "How old was Jamie when she discovered this very same style?"

For a moment, Lucas didn't answer, almost as though he understood the turmoil behind Danny's revolt, and then he smiled, falling in with Marianna's teasing diversion. "Jamie's my daughter," he said to Danny. "She's fourteen, a little older than you are, but she went through some pretty

hard times after her mom died. I thought that in spite of the
age difference, you two might find a few common interests
and that she should be the one to introduce you around. Instead of me, I mean,'' he added when he saw Danny's pend-
ing and instinctive refusal.

Danny subsided, silent but once again sullen. Meg wanted
to shake him, and she wanted to hug him. Instead, she looked
at Lucas who seemed to be waiting for some sort of answer.
Daughter, huh? Well, that answered a question she hadn't
even let herself ask. That was at least one reason why it was
Lucas Lambert, the sheriff, she would be seeing in the future.
Lucas Lambert, the man, obviously had enough to fill his
life, if he was raising a child alone. God knew she understood
how draining that could be.

And it answered or at least hinted at answers to some of
the questions she hadn't allowed herself to ask—about his
secrets, about his pain.

Meg found her smile, the cocky one the patrons at Patrick's had known and expected, and turned it on Marianna.
''Did you say aristocratic?'' she asked the woman, peering
down at her from an advantage of several inches.

Marianna nodded, acknowledging the role everyone in the
room understood Meg was playing.

''Well, then,'' Meg said, ''I suspect we'd better get busy.''

He came back. Later that afternoon when he was sure
Marianna would have finished the first phase of her new
assignment and when he hoped that Danny had taken himself
off to explore the rambling grounds of the estate.

There was no reason to return. Lucas told himself that as
he parked the Land Rover and strode across the lawn. Anything he had to say to Meg could be said by telephone, or
even relayed by a third party. There was no reason to think
she would even want to see him again, except for the memories of the way her eyes sought his whenever her new life
threw another obstacle in her path.

He found her in the garden, sitting on the sun-warmed
lawn beside the marble pool and fountain that so fascinated

his daughter. She had drawn up her knees to rest her chin on them and wrapped her arms around her legs.

And she was lost, staring unseeingly at something or somewhere far away from Avalon, New Mexico, and all the changes that an unwitting burglar had brought into her life. Was she missing the small duplex she had made into a warm, welcoming home? Or Patrick McBean, the man she'd told him had given her a job and hours that took into account her schooling and Danny, and reinforced the sense of self-worth Meg had spent a lifetime building?

A soft breeze found its way through the trees and teased a lock of Meg's hair across her cheek. Absently she brushed it back, sighed and raised her tented hands to her mouth. He noticed the sheen of moisture in her eyes. And she noticed him.

"No. Don't get up," he told her when she started to scramble to her feet. "I'm sorry I startled you." He crossed the few steps and seated himself on the stone ledge of the pond. "I'm sorry I disturbed you. You looked lost in thought."

Meg sniffed once and grinned up at him. "What a kind way of saying I was wallowing in my emotions."

"Were you?" he asked. "Wallowing?"

"Maybe." Meg looked, and for a moment all her indecision and confusion and pain flowed from her to him. "Have you ever had your life completely change, Lucas? I thought I had seen changes—as Danny and I moved from one town to another—but I always knew who I was and who my son was. Now I've learned that all of that was based on a lie so horrible I can't bear to consider it. Now I don't know who I am. I don't know who I can be. Can you have any idea how frightening that is?"

Oh, yes. He knew. He knew too well. But there was a difference in the changes she was undergoing from those he had been forced to make. "Do you have to know right now? Can't you give yourself time to explore the possibilities? It's only the outer trappings that have changed, Meg. Beneath all of those, you're still the same fine woman and mother you were yesterday. And Danny's still the same fine boy.''

She chuckled softly. "I hope so. I keep reminding myself to be patient, that this phase of his won't last long.''

''I'll send Jamie over tomorrow. She'll show him the town and introduce him to her friends. If nothing else, peer pressure will bring him around.''

Again she laughed. And this time she did rise to her feet with an innate grace she seemed completely unaware of. She dusted off her slacks and cocked her head to one side as she looked at him. "But that's not why you came. There's more, isn't there?''

Yes, there was more reason for his being here. More than he, himself, could even begin to understand. More than he could ever tell Meg Carlton. But this much he could tell her, even though he knew she wasn't ready, even though he'd like to shield her from this. He nodded. "The Bureau called.''

She paled slightly, then sank onto the ledge beside him. "And so it starts?''

''Soon, Meg. Soon.'' He pulled a sheaf of papers from the inside pocket of his suit jacket. "I've dictated a statement based on what you told me yesterday. If you'll sign it, I'll send it on to them. That ought to keep them quiet for a while.''

Meg took the pages. When she looked up from them, her eyes were bright with relief. "You kept it to the minimum.''

''That's all they need for now. Later, yes, they will ask more questions than you'll ever want to answer about your kidnapping. But this will keep them away until you've had a chance to orient yourself. And until you've had time to confer with the Carlton lawyers.''

''When?'' she asked.

''Tomorrow. Edward's personal attorney, Fallon Teague, is flying in late tonight. I'll delay this report as long as I can so that he can begin preparations before the Stemples or Blake are questioned—''

''Blake? Why would they question him?''

He heard the thread of panic in her voice, quickly masked, and cursed himself for causing it. "Even if they don't, Meg, he will hear the news when it's released. And it will be released. Or leaked. This was too big a case for someone to pass up the opportunity for publicity. But for now we've all agreed to play it low-key and quiet."

"You mean, not tell?"

He nodded.

"I— Then I guess it's a good thing I didn't tell Patrick any more than you did. I mean, about a family emergency taking me out of town. I...thank you for calling him last night, Lucas. I didn't think of it until very late. He's been a good friend to me. He deserved to know a lot more than just that I won't be back."

"And he will, Meg. In fact, I don't see any reason why you can't tell him...but Fallon might, so please wait until after you talk to him tomorrow before you begin contacting your friends."

"Lucas—"

The breeze once again caught a wayward curl and teased it across Meg's cheek. Without thinking, Lucas lifted his fingers to it and eased it back in place. He heard Meg suck in a startled breath before he realized what he had done, but by then it was too late. His fingers rested on her cheek. She closed her eyes and turned her face slightly, into his touch, before her eyes flew open and her mouth parted in a silent question.

Not now, he told himself. Maybe not ever. Meg Carlton was a warm and loving woman, and it would be too easy to take advantage of her confusion or even her gratitude in her present mood. Lucas commanded his fingers to move from the softness of her cheek, to reach instead for the statement she held gripped in one hand. "If you'll sign this," he said, "I can get it in tonight's mail instead of faxing it."

Yes. Confusion. He saw that in her eyes. And he saw her understanding of his delaying tactics, with her and with the FBI.

"Of course," she said, standing. "And tomorrow morning? You will be here, won't you?"

Was it a question or an order? Lucas couldn't be sure. It seemed this fragile-looking woman wasn't quite so unprepared to take her place in the Carlton empire as she thought. He shouldn't come back—Fallon was more than capable of guiding her through the morass of paperwork and protocol facing her—but he knew that nothing short of a major disaster would keep him from her side during this initial interview.

"Yes," he told her. "Yes, I will be here."

Four

Meg sighed with pleasure as the soft wool crepe settled over her body. Oh, yes. She could get to like this. She soothed the softly draping emerald green skirt in place and glanced in the full-length mirror in her dressing room.

She'd done easier things than that which she would be called upon to do in just minutes, but she'd done harder ones, too. It helped, a lot, that thanks to Marianna Richards and the experts she had called in, Meg now looked the part she was being called upon to play.

She touched her hair, not yet daring to disturb the new style. It was shorter than she had ever worn it, but feathered so that it looked longer and fuller. And it accented her eyes and cheekbones in a way that made her wonder if some fairy magic hadn't been at work on those, too, while she slept.

At a discreet knock on her door, Meg slipped her feet into the two-inch heels Marianna had insisted upon and which brought her height to an even six feet. Old tapes played hard and loud. She found herself wanting to kick off the shoes

and slump to hide her height. Instead, she threw back her
shoulders and lifted her chin.

Edward's housekeeper waited patiently in the hall. She
wasn't an unkind woman, or a suspicious one, just aloof.
Even though Jennie had affectionately referred to her as
Tommy, Meg hadn't yet figured out how to chip away any
of the woman's layer of strict professional decorum. "Okay,
Mrs. Tompkins," Meg said. "Lead me to the wolves."

The wolves waited in Edward's study, a wonderful room,
full of leather and dark polished walnut. There were three of
them, Fallon Teague and two men who accompanied him.
She studied them from the open doorway before entering the
room and easily identified Teague. She recognized the type
from the late-lunch crowd at Patrick's. Strictly Type A,
power lunch, constantly accessible either by cellular phone
or pager—except she didn't think that Fallon Teague would
stoop to carrying his own phone. No, one of the other two
would do that, as well as carry any necessary papers.

She searched for Lucas and, yes, found him standing in
the back of the room against one of the floor-to-ceiling bookcases. Her heart gave that funny little rush it had the day
before, when he had touched her cheek, and suddenly the
men in the room didn't seem nearly so intimidating. She
stared at Lucas until he shifted and turned slightly and saw
her in the doorway. His eyes acknowledged her presence as
a small smile—of approval?—softened the frown that had
darkened his face.

She took the one step that placed her in the room, and
Fallon and the two men looked up from the cluster of chairs
in front of Edward's massive desk.

Type A and suspicious.

She returned their steady appraisal.

First Fallon and then his associates stood. All remained
silent, as she did, waiting.... Waiting for what?

Finally a shadow of a smile rewarded her patience. "Miss
Carlton," Fallon said, "welcome home."

Meg sank into the deep leather chair beside the fireplace
in Edward's study after the men left. For a first meeting, it

hadn't been too bad, a few affidavits, a little uncomfortable conversation and, until Lucas had put a stop to it, a gentle probing by the attorneys about those events of twenty-five years ago that remained shrouded by the mists of time.

There would be more, much more, the next day and in the days afterward, as Meg resumed a life she had never dreamed of. As she did what she knew now she must do—protect Danny from the claims his father and even the grandparents who had turned their backs on him quite probably would make on him and his interest in the Carlton wealth if anything should happen to her.

But that would be tomorrow.

She glanced at the fireplace. Logs lay neatly stacked, compliments of another of the as-yet-unseen good fairies of her brother's house. Kindling beneath them just waited for a match. It was amazing, she thought. In only two days she had grown so addicted to the comfort of sleeping and waking with the lighted fireplace in her bedroom that it seemed almost a necessity. Should she light this one?

Why shouldn't she?

If she had been raised as Megan Carlton, would she have lit the fire? Or would she have summoned someone else to do it for her? It didn't matter. She was Meg Carlton. Oh, God, *she* was Megan Carlton.

She shook off the sudden fear that chilled her, and struggled up from the depths of the chair. An antique container on the carved walnut mantel held long, fireplace matches. She took one and knelt at the hearth. With only a bit of a fumble, she opened the damper, then lit the match, touched it to the kindling and sank back on her knees to watch the flames lick up and finally catch on the split firewood.

And if she had been raised as Megan Carlton, would she have met Lucas Lambert? Would he have stood in the back of the room looking solemn and somewhat foreboding in the dark gray suit and custom-made Western boots that seemed to be his working uniform while she conferred with more legal talent than most people ever met? Or would he have

done what she had wanted during that entire ordeal—walked
to her side and either taken her hand or placed his hand on
her shoulder?

"You look at home there."

He came back. Meg felt a smile building, all out of pro-
portion to his simple return, and turned her head to hide it
from him. "Do I? I was just wondering." *Now* she could let
him see her smile. "You're very good at that, you know."

"At what?"

"At catching me lost in my emotions."

"Were you?"

"No." Meg shook her head and looked up at him. "Unfortunately I knew exactly where I was, I just couldn't get
out."

Lucas leaned against the door facing and studied her silently for a moment. Then, as though he had made some sort
of grim decision, he nodded. "I think getting out of this
house for a while might help. Danny's busy, off with my
daughter. You have no more pressing responsibilities right
now. Come with me. I'll give you a tour of your new home."

When Lucas Lambert had first come to Avalon seven years
before, he had thought the town and the people in it insular,
snobbish and so far out of step that they would never be able
to catch up with the modern world. He'd also thought it his
penance to stay there for however long Alicia lingered in the
hell of pain her life had become. Jamie, his unexpected
daughter, had been his only consolation, and his only joy in
those first months.

He'd thought the offer of the office of sheriff a sop to his
pride and a slur on his training. But he had taken the job,
swearing to use that position as a way of shaking up Avalon's complacency and as a central location from which to
work, to help those who were too weak or too oppressed to
help themselves. Even though he still at times fought against
the smugness that Avalon periodically slipped into, slowly
the village had worked its magic on his frayed nerves, slowly
it had won him, and, in a sense, healed him.

As it had healed Jennie and then Edward.

As it would heal Meg.

Now he watched with quiet pleasure the open delight she took as they walked through this transplanted English village, which had so unexpectedly been planted in the forested mountains of New Mexico in the nineteenth century and had grown and survived.

The streets were bricked, not cobbled, and the houses were roofed, not thatched, and considerably larger than cottages, but there was a sufficiency of half timbers and plaster, of tiny multipaned windows, of towers and steeples and out-of-the-way shops, of prosperous, thriving mercantiles, of churches and their gardens and sedate, well-loved cemeteries, and of the homes that housed the wealth—the old but still-growing wealth—that supported it all. And of course, the people, who smiled and waved and called out friendly greetings to them but did not encroach the area of privacy his presence and Meg's strong resemblance to the once painfully private Edward Carlton granted her.

"It's wonderful," she said when their walk brought them back to the gates of Edward's drive. "But how on earth…"

That had been his question, had been everyone's question, on first meeting this town.

"A group of English lords on a grand tour in the last half of the eighteen hundreds," he said easily. "Second sons, some of them third sons. I suspect it was a last-ditch attempt by their parents either to teach them responsibility or to get them as far away as possible if they couldn't be civilized. Most of them returned home, but a few of them looked around this country and saw opportunities they would never have at home. They apparently had paid some attention during their expensive educations or they couldn't have made it work for them as well as it did. And apparently they weren't as uncivilized as their parents thought, because they couldn't bear to leave all of England behind them."

"Amazing. And their descendants still live here?"

He nodded. "And the descendants of the staffs these

young men had been raised to believe they needed in order to survive."

Meg gave a surprised little laugh. "These men really roughed it for the first few years then, didn't they?"

And that had been one of his first thoughts, too. He found himself laughing with her. That was easy to do. Maybe too easy to do.

"And your folks? Were they part of that illustrious group of settlers?"

"No." Now it was too easy not to laugh, because he knew her next question had to be, *Then what brought you here?* "No. Some of my folks had already been driven away from here before the Brits came, and some of them had gotten no farther than the East Coast in their immigration into this country."

"Interesting," she said. "So how on earth did you find this wonderful place?"

It was the same question he'd dreaded, just a more tactful version, and one he wasn't yet ready to answer to this woman, not even with his cleaned up, edited version. Maybe especially not with his cleaned up, edited version. "Are you hungry?" he asked. "It has to be past lunchtime."

She recognized the evasion. He saw understanding in her eyes of secrets kept and respected, gone quickly as she gave him a wry smile. "You bet. But I'm a little confused about the protocol. Since we missed lunch, do I have to cook it myself, or do I just snap my fingers and say, 'Food, minions!'"

"Neither," he said. "First you give me a moment to tell the staff where we're going, and then you snap your fingers and say, 'Food, Lucas!'"

She stopped in their slow walk up the driveway and shook her head. Her eyes were sparkling with humor and enjoyment. He reached for her hand and gave it a quick clasp—surely that much wouldn't hurt—and then seemed unable to release his contact with this vulnerable woman. She was just the right height. With only a step he could bring her against him. With only a step, he could fold his arms around her, slant his head and erase the questioning pout that marred her smile. With only a step—

"So... " He dropped her hand and moved that step—away. Confusion, frustration, rejection. Did he really see all that, or did he see only a reflection of what he was feeling? "Why don't I inform the staff—"

She took a quick, cleansing breath, but her smile returned. "Yes," she said. "Please."

Lucas took her to the Lodge, an English hunting lodge on the outskirts of Avalon. She and Lucas arrived well after the usual midday mealtime, but Norris Huxtable, the innkeeper, welcomed them warmly, showed them into the transplanted if somewhat corrupted version of an English men's club and seated them in a luxurious grouping of chairs and side tables near a massive stone fireplace. Meg settled into the leather wing chair and studied the room while Lucas excused himself to answer a telephone message that had been waiting for him when they arrived. Now she sat alone among the evidence of a wealth that wrapped her in comfort and security and quieted her with sensual delights.

A smile played across her mouth and teased a nervous need to laugh as she used a heavy sterling spoon to stir rich cream into equally rich coffee their host had poured into a bone china cup and set on the table beside her prior to retreating. Oh, yes, those younger sons had done exceedingly well, if the ambiance surrounding her was indicative of their influence, and she had no doubt that it was.

She still felt like a little girl playing dress-up with forbidden clothes and makeup, sure that she was going to get caught and sent to her room without supper but unable to tear herself away from the temptations the game presented. But she wasn't. She belonged here. And if she told herself often enough, if Lucas kept telling her, she might one day believe it.

She thought maybe she might believe anything Lucas told her.

And that frightened her almost as much as the unfamiliarity of her situation did.

It wasn't his badge, or maybe it wasn't just his badge, because when she was with Lucas, she managed to forget he was a member of the same profession that Blake and his father used to their advantage at every opportunity. No, her fear went much deeper. She'd learned long ago that the only one she could trust, the only one she could rely upon, was herself. Now Lucas made her want to believe that she had been wrong, that there was someone on whom she could depend, someone for whom she could care, someone who wouldn't use her caring as a weapon against her.

And how had that happened? He'd been nothing but professional and polite since she'd met him. He'd made no overture toward her, and he'd given no indication he'd welcome one from her. None, except that brief moment of contact in the driveway that afternoon. None, except the moment when he'd touched her cheek the afternoon before. None, except the moment of contact as he helped her from the car when they first arrived at Edward's house.

And she could have imagined each of those times.

Meg sighed and closed her eyes. She was so needy. So needy. And she hadn't even realized she was, until she was shown all that had been stolen from her—not the money, not the material possessions, but a family. A family who would have wrapped her in their midst, who would have loved her, who would have allowed her to love them, who would have helped her shield Danny from all the disappointments and pain he had suffered.

She heard voices from the hallway and dragged herself back to the room and the day and the company of the man she would not allow to catch her wallowing in despair again.

He looked grim and foreboding when he returned to her side, much as he had when she'd first seen him in the FBI interrogation room in Tulsa, but he smiled before he turned and began prodding the dying fire with a heavy cast-iron tool.

She'd lived with suspicion too long. "What's wrong?"

He shook his head, not actually denying that anything was wrong, but not answering her question, either. "It seems the Lodge is almost empty this afternoon. I've asked Norris if he'd mind having us served in here."

"What's wrong, Lucas?"

"Then you might want to call Patrick—"

"What's wrong, Lucas?"

Now he did turn toward her, still holding the fireplace tool loosely in his hand. "I'd hoped we'd have more time for you to settle in before this happened, but someone apparently couldn't keep his mouth shut. It seems you'll be the main story on the evening news. The major networks have already contacted my office looking for Edward for interviews and trying to locate you."

"Blake—"

Lucas thrust the tool back into its holder with enough force to rock the heavy stand. "He won't know. Not yet. Who and where you've been for the past twenty-five years is still being kept quiet until the Bureau can ask some questions. But it's only a matter of time until he does find out, Meg. He and everyone else in your past."

She couldn't keep the bitterness from her heart or from her voice. "Want to bet I'll see more familial love in the next few weeks than I've seen in my entire life?"

He knelt in front of her chair and lifted her chin until she met his steady appraisal. "I'll keep them away from you. Just say the word and they won't get closer than the county line."

And she couldn't keep the sheen of tears from her eyes— maybe because with him she sensed she didn't have to hide them. "Oh, Lucas. They can't hurt me any more than they already have. But Danny needs a father, and he can't understand why his grandparents wouldn't want him. He's vulnerable, so vulnerable."

"Sshh. Nothing's going to happen to you. And Danny's bright enough to see through words of love when there've never been any actions to support them—"

"But he—"

"Fallon will have the trust agreements you insisted on drawn up and in effect before the California cartel finds you."

His choice of words surprised a chuckle from her. "'California cartel'?"

He gentled his fingers on her chin and traced her jaw before releasing her from his touch. "And Edward knows too well the damage that the effects of greed can do to the emotions of a young boy. He'd never let it happen to Danny, even if by accident or intent they manage to get past the two of us. Danny has family now, Meg, family who will love him unconditionally, and not simply say they do because of what controlling him can do for them. And so do you."

Yes. Yes, she did. Meg blinked back the tears that threatened to become more than a sheen, that threatened to destroy the careful makeup Marianna had coached her through applying. And she had a champion greater than any she had once dreamed of in her girlish fantasies. Now she reached to touch him, laying her palm against his cheek.

He looked surprised, stunned almost, at the contact. He glanced at her hand and then at her brimming eyes. "It will be all right, Meg. I promise."

"I know," she said, believing him, because no one would dare antagonize the implacable strength she sensed in him. "I know."

A sound at the doorway intruded. Lucas glanced away and then stood as though grateful for the intrusion as their host wheeled a linen-draped table containing their lunch into the room.

It was late afternoon before they returned to Edward's house. After Meg had called Patrick and Mrs. Henson and told them the bare bones of her story, after she had received their good wishes and promised to telephone later with more information about where she would be and when she would see them again, she had not wanted to return to the house. She knew she would have to prepare Danny for the news story, and she knew that whatever waited for her still waited regardless of her physical location. But if she were not in the house, pacing and restless, perhaps it wouldn't seem so imminent, so threatening.

Finally, though, as the shadows began to lengthen, Lucas turned to her with a question in his eyes. She fought against reaching for his hand, drew in a breath and nodded.

Mrs. Tompkins told them that Danny and Jamie, who was waiting for her father to come for her, were downstairs in the game room. They found them there, sprawled in front of an overstuffed sofa, engrossed in a lively competition over a video game. Both looked up, but Jamie, as though tuned into the tension Meg felt, abandoned the game and rose to her feet.

"You haven't met my daughter yet, have you?" Lucas asked.

Meg shook her head. No, she hadn't. But there was no mistaking the girl's resemblance to Lucas in coloring and in height. She was tall and almost painfully thin, with the kind of bone structure that would pay her a fortune later in modeling fees, if she had the temperament and desire to go that route, but that now probably only earned her the nickname of "beanpole."

"No," Meg said. "But I'm happy to meet you, Jamie."

"And I'm happy to meet you." The girl came forward with an open smile, confident of her welcome, confident of her place in the world. Meg felt her own smile slip and fought to hold on to it. At Jamie's age she had been just as tall and just as thin, but that was where the comparison ended. She saw Lucas slip his arm over his daughter's shoulder and give her a quick hug. She tried to remember if anyone other than Danny had ever touched her that way, if anyone had ever greeted her with the loving acceptance, with the joy, that Lucas greeted Jamie.

Well, what difference did it make if no one had? That was all in the distant past. She was who she was because of and in spite of all that had gone on before. But, oh, God, who *was* she?

Danny swiveled around from the controls of the game.

"Hi, Ma." Still "Ma." Apparently he hadn't yet come out of the blue funk, even though she noted that he'd cleaned up his wardrobe some.

"Hi, kid." He'd hate it, but she couldn't resist walking to his side and ruffling his hair. With a glance at the big-screen television, she identified the game. It was one of Danny's favorites, one that she had often rented and played with him on weekends. "Who's winning?"

Danny grimaced, whether from the hand on his head or the question, Meg couldn't tell. She suspected it was a combination of both, and she suspected that he resented that his new friend, a girl at that, was beating him at a game he had long since mastered. "What's up?" he said instead.

Lots, Danny, lots, she thought, but she didn't say that. "Something we need to talk about. But finish your game first."

He slanted a glance at Lucas as he scrambled to his feet. "Nah," he said. "If Jamie and her dad need to leave, it's okay. I can play this anytime. There's a closet behind that wall that looks like a video rental place." And then he spoiled his studied air of nonchalance. "You'll come back, won't you, Jamie?"

"Jamie and her father aren't leaving right now, Danny."

"Excuse me."

Mrs. Tompkins stood at the door holding a cordless telephone and looking toward Lucas. "Mr. Carlton is on the telephone."

"Thanks, Tommy." Lucas crossed to her and took the phone. "For me or for Megan?"

"For you, sir."

With a glance toward her that could have been apology, but just as likely could have been anything else, Lucas lifted the receiver. "Yes, Edward. Yes. Yes, she knows. No. Yes, I have. Everything is in place. I understand. Right. Tell her— tell her the whole town is thinking of her, too."

Well, that was certainly informative, Meg thought as she stood with one hand on her son's tense shoulder.

Lucas grinned, and his voice lost its hard professional

edge. "You two have a lot more in common than you think, Edward. Yes, of course she would."

He held the phone out to her. "He wasn't sure you'd want to talk to him."

Edward Carlton wasn't sure that *she* would want to talk to *him?* Megan took the phone Lucas handed to her and sank onto the sofa. "Hello?"

"Hello. Megan." Her brother's voice was every bit as rich as she had remembered. But maybe not so confident. "I'm sorry I can't be with you right now."

"That's all right—"

"No. No it isn't. You need your family around you, and we'll be home just as soon as it's safe for Jennie to travel."

"How is she?"

"Resting. Her surgery's been postponed for a couple of days, but she's no worse. Matilda—that's her nurse—finally chased me out of the room. How are you?"

Amazing. With Jennie so ill, Edward had actually thought to ask about her. God, was she going to cry? "I'm—I'm adjusting."

He laughed. Not a big laugh, but a healthy chuckle that was full of understanding. "I can well imagine. And Danny? Is he *adjusting*, too?"

She glanced at her son who was trying to look as though he wasn't listening intently to every word. "In his own way."

Once again Edward chuckled, but when he spoke he became all seriousness. "I wish I could spare you the next month or so. The press will have a field day with this. The attention will be intrusive and painful, but soon something else will come along and then we'll be forgotten again."

He would know. What else could she say? "Yes."

"Fallon has kept me advised. The steps you requested are necessary, Meg. I—I should have suggested them myself. As for your other family, you know they will try to contact you as soon as the FBI questions them and they know who you are."

"Yes. Yes, I know."

"Do you want them to be able to?"

"I—I don't know."

After a moment of silence, he sighed. "I thought as much. I'm sorry, Meg. I'd make this easy for you if I could. Since I can't, I can at least make it safe. I've talked to Lucas. There is extra security staff in position. And if you want or need to leave, for any reason, we have several places and a company jet at your disposal. Just let Lucas know. He's a good man, Meggie. I don't know anyone I would trust more with your safety."

"I... " Yes, she was going to cry. "Thank you."

"Don't thank me yet. I've given a statement and promised that you will, too, in the next few days. Keep your spirits up, Meggie. I know you've got enough to worry about without outside interference, but right now there's not much we can do about it short of locking ourselves away from the world, and believe me, that's not all it's cracked up to be."

Five

"**M**om?"

Meg looked up to find Danny staring at her in alarm. Scared by the moisture she felt on her cheeks, he'd turned back into the loving and thoughtful son he had been until this last upheaval in their lives. "What's wrong?"

She switched off the telephone and placed it on the arm of the sofa, but she refused to wipe at the tears on her cheeks. She refused to give them any more importance than they had assumed. "What's wrong," she said gently, "is that you and I are about to be on television."

"Cool…" Danny's mouth opened in a silent "oh" as he realized the consequences. "But that means Dad— Was that what that call was about? Has he found us?"

She looked toward Lucas for guidance. Damn. Damn, damn, damn! She'd never looked for guidance before. Because it hadn't been there.

"No. No," she told her son. "Your Uncle Edward just wanted to make sure we were all right. But your father will

find us someday, Danny. I don't think we can avoid that
much longer.''

"But—"

Lucas stepped to the back of the couch and did what she
had wanted him to do for days now. He touched her. He just
rested his hand on her shoulder, but she felt his strength
flowing into her. She lifted her hand and placed it on top of
his.

"But he will never hurt you again, Danny," he said.

Danny looked at their joined hands, and his mouth twisted.
"My dad's a cop," he said, and Meg heard the belligerence
return.

"So your mom told me."

"Yeah. Well cops always believe other cops."

"No, Danny," Lucas said firmly. "They don't."

"What channel, Pops?" Jamie asked as she reached for
the remote control, but she, too, was looking at their clasped
hands.

Oh, Lord, had she overstepped the boundaries of what Lucas was offering? Quickly Meg withdrew her hand from his.

"I don't think it's going to matter," Lucas told them.

It didn't.

Jamie turned on the feature that let them preview other
channels while watching one, and they found Meg Carlton's
return was the lead story on each broadcast.

"Mom, is that—" Danny blurted out when the picture
dissolved to old file footage of a handsome, laughing couple
pushing an infant in a swing while a dark-haired, younger
version of Danny stood nearby bouncing a basketball.

"Yes. That's your mother in the swing," Lucas told him.
"With your Uncle Edward and their mom and dad."

"Wow, that's awesome." Danny swiveled around to face
her. "They really loved you, Mom. They really, really loved
you."

Meg's tears ran unchecked. Yes. They had. And each
other. And Edward. Their love had been a visible shield
around them until greed had destroyed it.

The story progressed from the wait for the ransom note to

the finding of the bodies on that bleak stretch of California coastline. She saw Edward change from a laughing boy to a too-old young man under the guardianship of an uncle who wanted control of the companies but not the child who owned them. He had been raised in an environment every bit as cold and unloving as that in which Meg had been deposited. No. Edward's substitute family was no better than Meg's—maybe even marginally worse. According to the story, his uncle was later indicted for embezzling from his young charge's estate. Then she saw the recap of the story she would have seen a year before, had she not been embroiled in a drama, minor—nonexistent—by comparison, of her own: Edward almost losing his new wife, and Jennie, a talented artist, losing six months of her life and ultimately her sight, if this new surgery were not successful, thanks to another kidnapper. Edward's second cousin had been involved and was now fighting a conviction of kidnapping, conspiracy and attempted murder.

Fairy tales always had a dark side. Meg had known that forever. She just hadn't known how dark they could be or how much danger could lurk in the deceptively secure lives of Avalon's residents. She twisted around to look at Lucas and in doing so lost the warmth of his hand on her shoulder.

With the loss of his touch, she also lost the warmth of his presence. "Other than taking ordinary precautions, I see no reason for either of you to alter your actions while you are actually in Avalon," he said, answering her unspoken question.

And she lost the warmth of his voice, because he was once again Lucas Lambert, the sheriff.

"Your household staff is specially selected and trained to cope with most emergencies, as is the staff of my department. But I would like for both of you to take classes in self-defense."

Danny threw out a stiff-armed fist and assumed a pose vaguely reminiscent of Chuck Norris. "You mean this stuff?" he asked excitedly. "Will you teach us?"

Lucas smiled at the boy but shook his head. "No.

Tommy?'' Only then did Meg realize that Mrs. Tompkins had not left the room. She nodded—some blasted shorthand that Meg wasn't privy to—and so did Lucas. ''Tommy will work your lessons around your daily schedule at the gym here in the house, Meg. But I think Danny might benefit from the classes at the department—''

Danny was all but bursting with enthusiasm for the new project, until Lucas added ''—that Jamie teaches.''

In the week that followed the news broadcast, Meg grew accustomed enough to her new hairstyle to feel free to run her fingers through it, and to her new makeup enough to be able to apply it in less than half the time it had taken at first.

She grew accustomed to Marianna's unassuming friendship as she guided Meg's own good taste through the intricacies of running a house the size of Edward's and just as gently guided her through the social history of the Carlton family.

But she couldn't quite get used to the luxury of having Mrs. Tompkins bring her breakfast tray to the sitting alcove in her room each morning, or to the necessity of that same reserved woman donning exercise gear and meeting her on a mat in the basement gym and teaching her, first how to defend herself and then how to do serious injury to anyone who tried to harm her.

She couldn't quite get used to the quiet, intense courtesy shown her by Fallon Teague, Davis Ryan and Kent James, his assistants, as they discussed trusts, property and amounts of money far beyond even her fertile imaginings.

And she couldn't quite get used to the loss of the one friend she had thought she had in this alien world. Although Lucas continued to attend her meetings with Fallon and to keep her up-to-date on the progress, or lack of it, in the Bureau's investigation and in the press's attempts to locate her, he remained clearly Lucas Lambert, the sheriff.

And she missed Lucas Lambert, the man.

She wouldn't let herself pursue that too closely, though.

Her track record with personal relationships was impressive only because of her failures.

Danny, at least, was having no problem with personal relationships. He came home from school daily with stories and names of the new friends he had met. He and Jamie had become almost inseparable during nonschool hours, but he steadfastly refused to let her teach him self-defense.

"She's a *girl*," he'd said as if that explained everything.

Meg didn't think it did. "So?" she'd asked.

"She'd be better than me."

"So?" she'd repeated.

"Mom!"

That was his I-thought-you-were-smarter-than-that tone.

"I might hurt her," Danny mumbled. Meg just cocked her head and waited. "Oh, well, heck," he said finally. "She'll throw me. I can't have a *girl* tossing me all over the exercise mat."

Meg hadn't insisted that he do so. Maybe she should have, she thought later, during one of the now-regular morning meetings with the attorneys. Lucas was seated at the small conference table across the room with Davis and Kent. Maybe she should talk to him—about an alternate teacher for Danny, but the danger to them didn't seem quite real, nothing seemed quite real, and the security around them was so strong.

"Meg?"

She looked up. "Yes, Fallon?"

"These papers are ready for your signature. If you'd review them now…"

If you'd review them now, we could get on to the next step in the never-ending steps we're going to have to take to bring you back to your world.

She rose from the chair and walked to the desk. "Of course."

He vacated the chair, and she seated herself and began scanning the pages of the document before her. This was the important one. This one protected Danny. With Fallon and his firm hovering in the background as an up-against-the-

wall backup, control went first to her, then to Edward and
Jennie, and then, if a disaster took all of them, to Lucas
Lambert until Danny was old enough to take charge himself.

Meg looked up to find Lucas watching her. "Is this all
right with you?" she asked.

"Yes."

As easily as that, he accepted this responsibility. As easily
as that, Meg trusted him. Yes. She turned to the signature
page and found all of her names listed there: Margaret Ann,
Meg, Megan Elizabeth, Carlton, Stemple and Wilson in all
of their varieties and possible combinations.

"This makes me sound like some sort of criminal," she
muttered as she signed the first name of the list to the one
line provided: Megan Elizabeth Carlton.

Megan Elizabeth Carlton. Megan Elizabeth Carlton. Megan Elizabeth Carlton. If she repeated that often enough,
maybe she'd finally believe that was who she was. There
was only one problem with that; after more than a week in
her new identity, she still hadn't a clue as to who Megan
Elizabeth Carlton really was.

There were other papers to sign. Fallon called Mrs. Tompkins and Marianna Richards, who had stopped by, into the
room as witnesses, but eventually each was signed and sorted
and neatly stashed in the briefcase carried this morning by
Davis Ryan. There would be more. It seemed as though there
would be a never-ending flow of documents, reports and proposals, but for now she had a brief recess. Fallon and his
men left. Marianna and Mrs. Tompkins left.

Only Lucas remained with her in the room. He'd stood
and walked to the fireplace. How strange. Usually he made
his excuses and left with Fallon.

Why hadn't he left?

"Lucas?"

He looked grim, but then, no more grim than usual since
he had become once again only the sheriff. Had he realized
what she had only begun to realize—that she needed a friend,
that she needed someone to spend her time with, to fill up
the empty hours in this new world, that she needed him.

"Fallon didn't mention it," he told her, "but we have been discussing your law school classes. It seems a shame for you to lose the entire semester, so Fallon spoke with the dean of your law school. If you wish—don't let us push you into something that you don't want to do, but if you wish, Fallon will assign one of his associates to tutor you through the remainder of the semester, and you will be allowed to complete it."

Well. It wasn't what Meg had hoped for, but it was something to fill up her time without Lucas having to be with her.

No, that wasn't fair. What Lucas had done was extremely generous, and she had no doubt that he was the one responsible for this minor miracle. Meg dredged up her smile, the one she had perfected on Patrick's customers. "Thank you," she said. "I appreciate your concern."

Damn! Lucas wasn't the type to kick tires; he hadn't been since he was ten years old and his father had impressed upon him the responsibility of caring for property. Only much later had he learned about the responsibility of caring for other people. But now, with the memory of Megan Elizabeth Carlton Wilson's polite dismissal still echoing in his ears and the memory of her polite and forced smile still clouding his vision, he was in the mood to vent unaccustomed anger on some inanimate object.

He'd thought Meg would be pleased with the opportunity to finish this semester. He knew how hard she'd worked to get as far as she had, and after that brief, enlightening conversation with her on the plane, he realized how brave she had been to get as far as she had. Yes, he knew that single parents worked all the time to earn college degrees and advanced graduate credit. But on the run? And with a background of being told that she was—*God!* had those people really told Meg she was dumb?

And maybe she was pleased, but if so, why did it feel as though he had just planted his size-twelve boot in the middle of her birthday cake?

His mobile phone chirped at him as he opened the door

to the Land Rover—chirped for God's sake. Whatever happened to good old healthy rings? But he didn't have time to ponder that question. Only the department and his daughter had the number for this telephone. He snatched up the receiver. "Lambert."

"Boss?"

It was Tully, his first deputy. "Yes. What is it?"

"You want to come to the station? We've got some information on those inquiries of yours."

Lucas Lambert and Trent Dawson went back a long way, longer in time and in distance than either of them wanted to remember, back to a time before the FBI and before the Avalon Sheriff's Department. With only few and notable exceptions, Trent was now more or less confined to the Bureau's D.C. offices, thanks to one bullet too many.

Lucas had felt no qualms about contacting his former partner for help in the investigation of Meg's kidnapping; Trent had voiced none about supplying that help. Apparently that kidnapping fell into the category of few and notable, because he'd assigned himself to the field interrogations.

When Lucas returned Trent's telephone call, he reached him at the Bureau's San Francisco headquarters. Trent wasted little time in pleasantries. "Has Ms. Carlton remembered anything that might help?"

Lucas swore briefly but succinctly. "She was three years old," he said. "What kind of help do your people expect from her after all this time?"

"Oh, names, addresses, complete descriptions, license tag numbers. Little things like that."

"Dream on. What about your end? How did the family react?"

"It was interesting. Except for the ex-husband, they weren't surprised. Oh, the Stemples put on a good act, but they weren't stunned, and they didn't ask the kinds of questions you'd expect about the welfare of a child they'd raised. In fact, I'd be willing to bet they knew who we were and why we were there from the moment we stepped onto their porch.''

So they weren't surprised, which meant that they must have had a suspicion that the little girl they took into their home wasn't just a homeless orphan. Oh, yes, James and Audrey had a whole lot to answer for. ''This was after the news release?''

''Yeah. And wouldn't I like to get my hands on whoever furnished that leak.''

''How do you read the ex?''

''He's not someone I'd want guarding my back, but then I never was partial to bullies. Especially bullies in uniform.''

''Then he's still a police officer.''

''Yes. A captain with the Simonville PD. His father is the chief of police. The chief insisted on being present while we questioned Wilson—said it was departmental policy, and it probably is, but there was a whole lot more than just departmental interest in that office. And there was definitely something going on. Wilson seemed almost relieved when we told him we were investigating a twenty-five-year-old crime.''

''Probably because that particular bully's favorite target is small children, specifically his small child.''

''Oh, hell. And his wife?''

''Not that she's admitted,'' Lucas told his friend. ''I know he practiced his intimidation techniques on her, maybe just emotionally and verbally, but I suspect he at least tried more.''

''How is she doing? The Tulsa agents told me she seemed pretty fragile.''

Lucas didn't even try to contain his smile. If those agents could see Meg as he had seen her during the past week, all color and style and flair and with her self-doubts masked by the aura Marianna had helped her build, they'd swear she was a different woman. But she wasn't. His smile slipped as easily as her mask had slipped that morning. And she was fragile.

''How is she doing?'' Lucas repeated. ''I think I'll use the

words she told her brother the day the story broke. She'
'adjusting.' ''

Trent chuckled. ''And I'll bet there's more to adjust t•
than even you or I could imagine.'' The humor faded from
his voice. ''We are going to have to talk to her in spite o•
your reports. And you know that her family and the pres•
will find her.''

''Yes.'' He'd known all he could do was delay the inev•
itable. ''So what's happening out there? Will you be talkin•
to the Stemples again, backtracking on the adoption, o•
what?''

''Yes, to all.''

''And keeping an eye on them?''

''Lucas.''

Lucas heard the simple warning. Trent might share som•
information; after all, they were involved in the same case•
But he wouldn't break departmental policy.

''Right. Well, I think I'll keep an eye on them. Paul Slate•
does investigative work for the Carlton enterprises. Do yo•
have any objections if I give him a call?''

''Would it matter if I did?''

Would it matter? Only if it destroyed their friendship. Bu•
even that wouldn't stop him. ''No.''

''I thought not. So, speaking of stubborn, how's my favorite honorary niece?''

Lucas chuckled. ''Taller. Brighter. More inquisitive. And
Lord, Trent, she's going to be gorgeous.''

Money didn't always corrupt, Lucas thought as he replaced the telephone receiver and questioned the course o•
action that his mind had immediately presented him. He'd
always given lip service to believing that money itself was
inanimate, incapable of inflicting pain, but he hadn't really
believed until after he'd traced Alicia to Avalon, after he'd
met Reverend Winthrop, after he'd met Marianna Richards's
father and his group of friends, men who felt as Lucas did:
that money was a tool to be used, not a god to be worshiped.

But it did corrupt. Otherwise, the uncle who had been
entrusted with the care of Edward Carlton after his parents'

deaths would have been more concerned for the boy than with the fortune placed at his disposal. Otherwise, the man who had sired Lucas would have cared enough for his wife to notice that her inability to function as the hostess and ornament he required was caused by a deep-seated illness. Otherwise, he would not have treated his sons like pawns to move around on the chessboard of his business enterprises. And otherwise, Lucas himself would not have awakened at age thirty to find that the core of his own character was so black with the kind of selfishness that could only have been built up, layer after layer, year after year, that only separating him from all aspects of his past could give him any hope of redemption. And even that hadn't been enough.

No, money didn't always corrupt. But greed for it could, did and would. And what Megan had suffered at the hands of those who should have loved her, who should have cherished her, would only be a prelude to the pain they could now cause her, if he read their characters correctly.

In the past several days he'd told himself more often than he cared to think about that Megan didn't need him in any capacity other than as guardian of her and her son's physical safety. Had he been lying to himself then? Or was he lying to himself now to justify doing what he'd wanted to do all along?

He found Meg in the dining room of her brother's house. He couldn't miss seeing her welcoming smile as she looked up from her solitary lunch, and he didn't miss the wistful little sigh she gave before she dimmed her smile. Tommy followed him into the room and stood by the doorway. Meg gestured toward the chair across from her. "Will you join me for lunch?" she asked.

"No. No lunch," he said as he walked around the table and took the chair next to her.

"Would you care for some coffee, then?" she asked. "Or tea? Mrs. Tompkins, would you please—"

But Tommy had already moved toward the sideboard

where she poured coffee into a delicate cup. "Thanks Tommy," he told her when she served it to him.

"Will there be anything else, sir?"

He felt Meg's steady regard as he declined further help from her housekeeper, but she remained quiet until after Tommy had left the two of them alone. "Sometimes I wonder just who she works for. Edward? Or you?"

Her words were lightly spoken, but Lucas heard in them the same bravado he had first heard in the Tulsa interrogation room.

"Technically, she works for Edward."

"But reports to you?"

"Only when Edward is not available."

"I see." Meg concentrated on stirring her coffee. "And what brings you back for the second time in one day, Sheriff?"

Ouch. It seemed he had been more successful than he thought in distancing himself from Megan Carlton. Well, this was after all an official call. And he doubted very much that she did *see*.

"Finish your lunch, Meg. There's plenty of time to discuss why I came back."

She pushed back from the table and stood. "I'm finished." In what he knew had to be a deeply ingrained habit, she reached for her plate. Giving a little sigh, she left it on the table, straightened and turned toward him. "Shall we go into the study?"

Yes, Meg was *adjusting,* but she certainly wasn't comfortable with her new life. Would she ever be? Leaving her alone in a strange house with nothing but lawyers and unknown staff couldn't be helping, because he recognized in her voice and her actions more than wistfulness, bravado, distance and habit. He recognized loneliness: bone-deep, soul-deep loneliness. Recognized it. Oh, hell. Recognized it because it ran just as bone deep, just as soul deep within him.

"Why don't we go for a drive instead?"

For the first time that day, he saw animation and excitement in Meg's eyes. "Could we?" she asked.

"Yes." Oh, yes, they definitely could. To keep that excitement in her eyes, he'd take her damned near anywhere and count the cost later. Much later. "But you'll need a jacket. It's getting chilly."

Six

Meg found Marianna waiting in her sitting room, ensconced on the small sofa with a sketch pad and a notebook. For a moment, poised in the doorway with Marianna unaware of her presence, Meg glimpsed in the woman a sadness as great as—no, deeper than—the one that so often lately had ambushed Meg.

Marianna glanced up and saw her, and the sadness vanished so quickly Meg couldn't be sure she had actually seen it.

"Aren't these great?" Marianna asked. "They came while you were at lunch. I knew you'd be as excited about them as I am."

These appeared to be a double closet full of clothes and intimate apparel to complement the double closet full that had already arrived. Meg blinked and tried to clear her mind of the impression of her being suffocated under a pile of silk and wool being packed down over her by mountains of paper that Fallon Teague kept throwing on the pile. "Ah…"

Marianna stilled her hand on the garment bag nearest her. "It's a bad time for you. I'm sorry."

"No." Meg hurried to reassure the woman who had been nothing but gracious to her in her confusing new surroundings. "No, there's no reason to be sorry. It's just that Lucas—Sheriff Lambert—wanted to...to talk about some of the new developments in my—in my—"

Marianna graced her with a dazzling, warm smile. "We can do this anytime it's convenient for you."

"Now I'm the one who's sorry."

"Megan," Marianna said with a seriousness Meg had never suspected in her, "I would die for Lucas Lambert, maybe even kill for him. Rearranging my schedule is so low on my list of debts to him that I can't even consider it an inconvenience."

Meg's new wardrobe contained nothing so mundane as a simple jacket. With Marianna's help, she chose a soft wool cape the color of hammered brass to complement the deep sapphire blue of her dress. Then, hating to leave with Marianna's cryptic words hanging unexplained between them, but being practically pushed out of her room, Meg hurried to meet Lucas in the entry hall.

Escape.

That thought brought her to an abrupt halt at the bend in the stairway landing. Escape? From this elegant...prison?

Did she really want to go back to that tiny duplex in Tulsa, to rented furniture and thrift-store housewares that could be left without regret, to scrimping and saving, to being always on the run from a threat that might never again find her and Danny?

No. No, of course she didn't.

What she wanted was...was someone who had known her before she had begun her transformation into Meg Carlton, someone whose knowledge of who she was and who she had been would keep her anchored in reality. Lucas, no matter how briefly, had known her as Meg Wilson. He'd seen how she lived. He knew she'd had her own identity.

Maybe if she'd had time to devote to the developing friendship she felt with Marianna, maybe if Edward hadn't had to leave so that she had more of her brother than his nightly telephone calls in which he told her about a childhood she didn't remember—

Jennie. Oh, Lord. Was that why Lucas had returned? Had something happened to Edward's wife?

Lucas stepped into sight in the foyer below her and looked up. The harshness of his face softened slightly as he gave her an echo of a smile. No. Nothing horrible had happened. Lucas wouldn't smile, not even in that reluctant little way, if anyone in his care had come to harm.

In his care. Yes, of course. She kept forgetting that she was in his care. Nothing more. She shook her head. Lucas Lambert as protector was more than she'd ever had any right to hope for. Why, then, wasn't it enough? It was, she told herself. It was.

"Are you ready?" he asked from the foyer below her.

Was she? Hadn't she always had to be? "Yes," she said. Draping her cape over her shoulder the way Marianna had shown her, she lifted her chin. "I'm sorry if I kept you waiting."

Was he out of his mind? Lucas cast another quick glance at Meg, looking so right as she sat beside him, even if she was bristling like a hedgehog, before he forced his attention back to the street and his driving. Or had he been there for more years than he cared to count?

No. No, damn it! This was a business meeting. Nothing more. He had to remember that. This was a time to talk about Blake and the Stemples, the investigation and Meg's safety.

Then why did having her alone in the car with him, away from everyone and everything else that complicated their lives, feel like so much more? And why did he feel as though he had caused the hurt she was trying so valiantly to mask?

Enough! Her pain, physical and emotional, was the reason he had returned to the Carlton house; it was the reason he had invited her away from the house so that they might have a private moment to talk; and it was a reason he must not forget.

"Tommy tells me your lessons are not going well."

Meg's chin jutted up another notch. "She talks too much."

"It's her job."

"What? Reporting on my activities?"

He let that comment pass in silence as he deliberately studied the intersection at a four-way stop. Meg was entitled to a time to verbalize some of the turmoil she must be experiencing. Danny had been acting out his emotions almost since the moment he had learned of his mother's past. But except for those too few, too brief moments Meg explained away as having been "wallowing" in her emotions, she had kept all of her reactions to the upheaval in her life strictly under control.

All right; he had a solution for that. And if she wanted to pick a fight with him, so much the better—at least for this one time. With his decision made, he turned toward his house.

"She says you're holding back in your practice."

Meg twisted to look at him. "I'm five inches taller and ten years younger than she is. What does she expect?"

"You can't hurt her."

"Ha! Do you really expect me to believe my housekeeper is Bruce Lee reincarnated? Anyone can be hurt."

"Yes." Lucas allowed her to see his small, grim smile. "I didn't say she couldn't be hurt. I said *you* couldn't hurt her."

Meg's eyes widened slightly, but he saw the moment she decided not to open that can of worms.

"And I'm seriously supposed to try?"

He didn't answer her. Instead he drove silently, contemplating what he was letting himself in for. He'd avoided being the one to train Meg. Now he was just as deliberately forcing her into the physical contact neither one of them needed.

"Lucas," Meg said insistently. "Am I seriously supposed to try to hurt Mrs. Tompkins?"

He drove through the white brick gateposts that guarded the "new" subdivision of once again stylish art deco homes where he lived before he answered. "You're supposed to protect yourself, Meg. If that means hurting someone in order not to be hurt, then, yes, you're seriously supposed to try."

His house sat at the end of a cul-de-sac, far back from the street in a wide lawn with careful landscaping to set off the stark simplicity of the house. Jennie had pronounced it beautiful, even though he'd known she preferred the overgrown, romantic, security-nightmare garden of her own home.

"Oh." Meg leaned forward against her seat belt when he pulled into the driveway. "It's wonderful," she said as he pulled to a stop in the turnaround at the back of the house. "Who lives—"

He tugged the keys from the ignition and turned to look at her. If there were another way to do what had to be done today, he wasn't strong enough to find it. "Jamie and I live here. Come on inside. We have things to discuss."

As invitations went, Lucas's lacked a little in the warmth department. Meg grimaced as she stepped from the car, not waiting for him to open the door for her. It lacked a lot, and it lost even more when he saw that she hadn't waited for him to do his chivalrous thing with the door.

Well, what did he expect? She'd seen more warmth from hostile health inspectors who swore they didn't have a quota for restaurant demerits but acted as though they did—and had to meet it all in one business.

But the house was lovely, with clean, spare lines and a simplicity of design that attested to the craftsmanship and talent that had gone into its creation.

She didn't have much time to admire its beauty, though. She only glimpsed tall, white, glass-fronted cabinets in a sparkling kitchen before Lucas tugged open a door and led her downstairs to an equally sparkling exercise room. He went directly to a closet on the left, reached into it and turned, holding a shapeless white cotton practice suit like the one Mrs. Tompkins insisted on wearing, but that Meg had so far resisted in favor of a pair of familiar, comfortable sweats.

"This is Jamie's," he said, thrusting the suit into her arms. "But it ought to fit you." He nodded to a door on the far wall. "You can change in there."

"Just like that?" Meg demanded. "Don't I have any say in whether I want a lesson or not?"

"No," he said. "You don't."

In his care? Had she really thought that, only minutes earlier? She wasn't in Lucas's care; she was under his power. And she wouldn't tolerate that from anyone. Not again. Not ever again. "How interesting," she said, drawing herself up to her full height and putting as much chill into her voice as she could. "I would never have thought you were a bully."

Lucas remained unfazed, except for a slight narrowing of his eyes. "And I would never have mistaken you for a fool. But whether you change or not, you're going to get a lesson."

"Why?" Meg demanded. "Why now? Why so suddenly? And why you, when you've done everything you can to avoid me except when you've thought it was absolutely necessary to be there?"

Lucas turned away from her and calmly took his own practice suit from the closet. "Because as of yesterday," he said, "Blake and James and Audrey know who you are and probably by now where you are. And if they know, God alone knows how many nuts and fruitcakes also know. Because," he said, "there is no rationing of terrorism, and lightning can strike twice. And because," he added, slamming the closet door, "you won't practice properly because you are afraid *you* are going to hurt someone."

He stood facing the closet door, and she saw his shoulders flex and strain as he drew in a deep breath. "You can change clothes or not," he said with a calm that the tension visible in his body denied. "But I'm going to. And when I return to this room, we *will* have a practice session."

She changed. With trembling hands, she struggled out of soft wool into starched cotton and returned to the outer room. An exercise mat dominated the center of the room, but she spotted a padded bench along the wall near the stairway and sank onto it.

Blake knew. James and Audrey knew. They'd be here as soon as they learned where she was. Meg had no doubt about that. And neither had Lucas. But why had he thrown his knowledge at her like...like a weapon?

Blake knew. Oh, Lord. And he would be here. Danny. She had to take Danny and run. She couldn't let him hurt her son again.

"Meg?"

A hand clamped on her shoulder, and she jumped.

"Meg."

Lucas. It was only Lucas. She was safe. The tension whooshed out of her and just as quickly returned. Whatever she felt around Lucas Lambert, it wasn't *safe*. And right now, she was more than angry with him. She glared at his hand until he released her.

"You could have told me," she said.

He didn't pretend to misunderstand. "I just did."

She whirled around to face him and faced instead the broad expanse of his chest covered in his white cotton exercise suit. The unisex costume was anything but shapeless on him. It wasn't snug, and it wasn't confining; that would have defeated its purpose. But it did define the width and breadth of his chest and shoulders, the length of his leg and his narrow waist, belted now with a white quilted cotton sash he'd done a much more respectable job of tying than she had.

Lucas Lambert was a big man. Meg often forgot that because he had been unfailingly gentle with her. But after seeing him today, she didn't think she'd ever forget again. A big man. A massive man. A dark, unsmiling man.

Whatever sharp comment she'd been about to make died forgotten in her throat. She swallowed back what she recognized as an unfounded spurt of fear.

I would die for Lucas Lambert. Unbidden, Marianna's cryptic words floated to the forefront of Meg's memory. A man who could inspire that kind of loyalty couldn't be a danger to her. A man who could be as unfailingly gentle as Lucas had been until this afternoon *wouldn't* be a danger to her. Meg knew that; she was just having a little trouble remembering it. Especially when he looked anything but gentle as he loomed over her.

She scooted down the bench until she could stand and rose to her full height. It wasn't enough. Without the added inches of her heels she still had to look up to him. And he still loomed.

She thrust out her chin. "So what exotic martial art are you teaching me today?"

He stepped back and studied her. "I don't think you're ready, emotionally or mentally, for an eastern discipline." He nodded toward the mat. "So I think we'll concentrate on street fighting, down and dirty, with a few eastern surprises."

She managed a cocky grin. "Down and dirty? Is that based on an appraisal of my character?"

He didn't smile. "No. On an evaluation of your attitude today." He nodded again toward the mat.

Meg drew her shoulders up and marched toward the mat. There, she whirled to face him. "Okay. Do your best. I have to warn you, though, I already know a little about fighting dirty. I had to learn it the hard way. And if this new life of mine means I have to learn more, I'm not sure I'm going to like it here. But come on. Teach me how to hurt you."

He refused to be baited. He walked to the edge of the mat and looked at her calmly, but still grim and unsmiling. "The purpose of these sessions is not to teach you how to hurt someone, but to teach you how to keep from being hurt. Your best weapons are your mind, your voice to call for help and your legs to run as fast as you can away from a potentially dangerous situation. What I'm going to do, and what Tommy would have done if you'd let her, is teach you how to claw, bite, gouge and kick, in order to escape."

He wouldn't hurt her. Lucas wouldn't really hurt her. At

least not physically. Meg knew that at a level so deep within
her she didn't have to question it. But he was hurting her on
another level, one she didn't understand and couldn't stop to
explore. He had no idea that he was doing so, and that hurt
even more.

"You are, are you?" She held her hand toward him in
derisive invitation. "Then come on, Chuck Norris. Give it
your best shot."

He bowed slightly, and for the first time he smiled. Tight,
knowing, secretive. And it was the only thing she saw before,
with a speed and grace she would never have suspected, Lucas lunged for her. It was the only thing she saw before she
found herself seized in an embrace that had nothing to do
with affection and everything to do with the flood of memories that assaulted her: Blake, when she had tried to pull
him from Danny the time that had finally made her take her
son and run; Audrey Stemple, the adoptive mother who
should have loved her but who poked and pulled and pushed
and shoved and used her greater strength to impose her will
on a child who only wanted to be loved; and another dark,
deep fear that only came in the middle of the night to ambush
her with a terror that left her chilled and sweating in the
aftermath of its assault.

Too much. It was too much.

To the accompaniment of her silent scream, Meg twisted
in Lucas's arms. As she launched her own attack with nails
and knees and elbows, she felt the give of Lucas's cheek
beneath her fingernails, but that was the only thing about
Lucas that gave. At some level Meg knew that the only force
Lucas used was to restrain her, not to hurt her. At some level
she knew that all she had to do to end his control of her was
to stop, to tell him calmly to release her. At some level she
knew that her fear and anger and frustration were coming
from something and sometime and someone other than here
and now and him. At some level. But not the one that kept
her twisting and struggling and striking out to the accompaniment of those awful sounds she heard.

She kicked out at him and lost her balance. Then both of

them were on their knees on the mat, still locked in combat. The sounds she heard were her own, shocking her almost to silence as she recognized the deep, agonizing sobs coming from her, *her,* when she never cried, never gave in to the weakness of even silent tears, never let anyone see what little distress she allowed herself to feel. And Lucas was still holding her, but not in restraint. Now his hands moved over her back, comforting her, shielding her, sharing his strength with her.

She wanted to tell him that she never allowed herself this weakness, but when she looked into his eyes, she realized she had no need to say anything. He knew. He knew. Lucas, who had known her for only a few days, knew more about her than the couple who had raised her, the man who had lied in his promise to love and cherish her, the brother who had lost her.

Lucas, this battered warrior with eyes that seemed to see through to her very soul, knew *her,* as no one else ever had. Yes. And with that knowledge, all the shame, all the embarrassment she had felt, all the need to hide the doubting, insecure, frustrated emotional wreck she too often was, fled.

Lucas knew from the moment he touched her that he shouldn't have. Meg was not a woman to be pushed; not by anyone, and especially not by him with his misguided ideas of helping her.

Helping her? God! What horrors had he opened for her? He'd only meant to give her the freedom to vent her emotions, but she fought like a woman possessed. It had taken all his skill to keep her from hurting herself, and him, in her frantic efforts to escape whatever pursued her. He had felt the sting as her nails drew blood on his cheek. He could have stopped her, he knew. With little effort, he could have immobilized her so that she was incapable of movement, but would that only have driven her further into panic?

"Oh, Meg," he murmured to her, folding her now in the embrace he had wanted to share with her since the day he had met her. But not like this. Never like this.

"Meg," he repeated, more firmly as he tightened his arm around her. Frail. God, she seemed so frail beneath the starched white cotton *Gi*, so delicate with her soft unbound breasts pressed against him, so lost as her whimpers turned to deep, soul wrenching sobs and the fight went out of her.

She curled against him, twisting her hands into the front of his *Gi* as though to hold him to her. Didn't she know there was no way he'd leave her alone with her grief? No. She probably didn't. That thought sobered him, and he forced his thoughts away from how right she felt in his arms, how perfectly her body fit against his, how much he wanted this embrace to have begun for another reason and to go on forever. He was absolutely certain that since she was three years old, Meg had had no one to share her grief, that until Danny, she'd had no one to share her joy; and he was certain too, that she had allowed no one before him to see her pain.

He loosened his hold on her, allowing her the freedom to move if she wished. But he was unable to resist soothing his hands over her shoulders and back, and he was unable to resist resting his cheek against her soft, feathered hair.

She didn't pull away.

Not at first. Not until her sobs faded. Then she squirmed in his embrace. Then she released her grip on his *Gi*. Then she ducked her head and swiped at her tears as though they were something shameful. And then she looked at him with her soul in her eyes, and he could hear the words of apology forming in her mind. Didn't she know he knew she had never been allowed to share her emotions with another person? Didn't she know he knew she had always had to be strong and capable and appear to be unfeeling? Didn't she know he would never violate the trust she had given him by allowing him to see her this way?

No. Of course she didn't know. And there was no way he could tell her without bringing even more embarrassment and discomfort to this proud, graceful, gentle woman. And there was no way he could do what his heart and his body urged him to do, no way he could force his attentions on her while she remained so vulnerable. No way he could kiss away the tears that washed her cheeks and the insecurity and confusion that clouded her eyes.

There was no way he could be anything but the sheriff, her brother's friend, the man who was supposed to be teaching her to protect herself.

Her mouth lifted in a tremulous smile; her hand lifted to grace his cheek. He closed his eyes when he saw a reflection of his own desire in hers. It was only vulnerability, he told himself, a reaction to the stress of the past week and of the emotional catharsis she had just gone through. There was no way she felt the same as he did, no way—

He felt the brush of her lips against his, and there was nothing tentative or vulnerable about the way they felt. Nothing tentative or vulnerable about the way Meg moved closer to him. Nothing tentative or vulnerable about the hunger and the need he sensed in her. Nothing tentative about the way his own hunger and his own needs met hers.

Oh, hell.

As natural as breathing. As necessary as breathing.

Meg felt Lucas's start of surprise as her lips touched his, and then she was where she had wanted to be, had needed to be, for longer than her conscious memory, in an embrace that was more right, true and real that she had any claim to, in an embrace that healed and filled all the empty caverns in her heart.

She felt the brush of the mat as he lowered her to it, felt the weight of Lucas against her, felt the tangle of their legs and the strength of cotton-covered muscle beneath her hands. She felt a need that she'd never before given freedom to demanding freedom, taking that freedom, as Lucas took control of the kiss she had begun.

Desire. Had she ever really felt it before?

And more. Much more. Every nerve ending she possessed had sprung to life, demanding…demanding something she had never believed in until this moment.

And accepting. Accepting the need and the demand she felt coming from Lucas. Yes. Need. A need as great as her

own. Meg didn't know how she knew, but she did; Lucas
needed her touch, her caress, *her,* as much as she needed
him.

Had anyone other than Danny ever needed her? Had any
one ever wanted her? Had anyone ever *cherished* her—Lu
cas's word, not hers, because she could only have dreamed
of this happening, never truly imagined it—as Lucas now
did with every touch, every breath?

Had anyone ever cherished him? She let herself wonder
that again, only briefly. She could. She would. She did.

She felt the rapid beat of his heart against hers and the
heat of his body beneath her hands. So little separated them,
only a fold of heavy cotton, but suddenly that was too much.
Meg longed for the touch of him, for the feel of his sleekly
molded muscle, for…for something that hovered just past
the edge of her knowledge…something that for the first time
in her life was almost within her grasp. With fumbling hands
she reached for the sash that was all that separated her from
that touch.

Lucas was lost in her, in the silken slide of her feathered
hair beneath his fingers, the softness of her cheek, the press
of her breasts against his chest, the tangle of her long, long
legs with his, the hunger that without guile or pretense she
let him see, let him share, the soft murmurs of encourage
ment and pleasure. Lost in a way he never thought he would
be. Lost, with the one woman he never thought he'd meet—
one that could see him, flawed though he was. Him. Not what
he could do for her. Not who he had been. God. One who
might even be able to forgive him for who he had been.

Who he had been. What he had done. What it had cost.

Too much. Too much for him ever— He pushed at that
thought, willing it away, as Meg turned in his arms, burrow
ing impossibly closer. Pushed at it, willing it to go, and it
almost did, until he felt her hands on his belt.

Reason and sanity descended in a rush, even though his
body was far from willing to welcome them. His belt, symbol
of the discipline he had told Meg that she didn't have. Sym

ool of the help he was supposed to be giving her. Symbol of the training and control he had worked years to develop. Control? He'd lost it like a testosterone-loaded boy when she'd touched him. And instead of helping her, he was taking from her. Damn his selfish soul to the hell where it already was; all he ever did was take.

With a groan, he captured her hands, stilled them and finally moved them from between them.

She looked at him with eyes clouded by desire and confusion, and he felt something in him rip and cry out. "I'm..."

Meg's expression shuttered. She shook her head against the mat, and then, without warning, rolled away, turning her back to him as she sat up and hugged her knees. "Don't you dare say you're sorry."

"Meg..."

"Just hush, Lucas." He heard the quaver in her voice and knew she fought tears. "Just hush."

He could do that. He could give her the time and space to compose herself. He owed her that much. He pulled himself to his feet, walked across the room and braced his hands on an exercise bar, fighting for his own composure.

He heard the whisper of fabric, followed in seconds by the click of the dressing room door closing, and sagged forward, closing his eyes and leaning his head against the wall. He'd never told himself the life he'd been given would be easy—it had cost too much—but he hadn't realized it was as empty as he now knew it to be, given the promises he had just glimpsed.

Meg gave herself one last look in the mirror. There wasn't anything in that tiny little bag of tricks that posed as a purse to help hide the ravage that tears and the last little foray into baring her heart and leaving herself wide open to rejection had done to her face. She supposed she had already embarrassed herself enough that the evidence of that embarrassment shouldn't hurt too much more. Still, she pressed a dampened washcloth to her eyes and held it there long

enough to take away the worst of the swelling, but not lon
enough—it would never be long enough—to take away th
hurt.

Finally, though, she donned the costume Marianna ha
helped her select, ran a comb through her hair and picke
up her cape.

Lucas was waiting for her in the outer room. Perfectl
groomed with his rich, dark hair, his impeccable gray sui
his elegant black Western boots, he looked once again th
sheriff, unapproachable, untouched.

No. Not quite. Meg saw a wariness in his eyes she ha
never noticed before. What did he think she was going t
do? Break down and sob like she had before or, worse, attac
him again? Well, he didn't have to worry about either o
those things—not ever again. Megan Elizabeth Margaret An
Carlton Stemple Wilson, whoever the hell she was, had to
much pride to subject either one of them to that embarras
ment again.

She wrapped the cape around her like the armor sh
wished it was and lifted her chin. "It's time to take me bac
to my brother's house. On the way there, you can finis
telling me about James and Audrey, and Blake."

She saw his eyes darken in protest at her brisk tone. Wel
what did he expect? He had already dismissed her by re
turning to his sheriff's persona. She lifted a hand to silenc
him. "And then I think you'd better contact the FBI. I
they're going to interview me, I want it to be soon. Now
Because I'm tired of being in limbo. I want it over with, s
that maybe, one day, before too long, I can have my lif
back."

Seven

___

Meg sat alone in the breakfast room holding a rapidly cooling cup of tea. The afternoon sky outside darkened with the threat of an early winter storm, making the day as bleak as the week that had just passed. Years of studying at a kitchen table had spoiled her for desks and offices, so when her books arrived the day after she'd voiced an interest in them—waved her magic wand, she thought wryly—she had chosen this usually cheerful little room with its three walls of windows as her retreat.

Now she had her texts spread out around her, trying to concentrate on contract law in the hour or so she had before the FBI descended on her for their too-long-postponed interview. At least contract law was constant, logical and so slow to change it seemed unchanging, because nothing else around her was.

In spite of her avowal to reclaim her life, in spite of her going through the motions—talking with Edward each evening; studying to make up the time lost in her classes; working out with Mrs. Tompkins each morning; working with

Danny to help him understand the changes in *his* life; with
Marianna to acquire the polish everyone seemed to think a
Carlton needed and that Marianna alone thought she already
had; and working with Fallon on the interminable paperwork
necessary to reinstate Megan Carlton and to protect not necessarily her but the wealth that was hers—she hadn't re-
claimed her life.

She and Danny had attended church with Marianna the
morning before in a quaint gray stone building straight out
of a Jane Austen novel.

Jamie had been at church, but Lucas hadn't. He'd been
working, Jamie told them.

Lucas.

Meg felt a swift rush of embarrassment. It was just as well
he hadn't been at church. She had a difficult enough time
facing him here, where and when it was necessary, without
the added burden of trying to hide her shame in a place
where too many people were all too curious about the new
resident of their town.

She set down her cup and clasped her hands, tight, beneath
her chin. She couldn't believe she had thrown herself at Lucas the way she had. Or maybe she could. How had she
described herself to Lucas when she had been trying to explain her attraction to Blake—tall even then, all arms and
legs and knees and elbows and so hungry for affection...

And she still was. Hungry. Needy. She could admit that
to herself if to no one else. But she didn't have to act on it.
She'd spent most of her life paying for the last time she had.

Lucas wasn't Blake. She knew that. She'd known that
probably since the first day she met him. If she hadn't, she
knew now. He hadn't taken advantage of her blatant offer of
herself, hadn't pretended to care about her, hadn't forced
himself to pretend to want what she offered. And he
wouldn't. He'd proven that in the days since. Even though
they were thrown together daily, he maintained a distance
and dignity she almost envied, a distance and dignity that—
almost—allowed her to maintain her own.

She heard the spatter of rain on the window and looked

up. Most of the leaves had already fallen from the trees—
she had no idea if it was late or early for that to have happened here in this isolated and otherworldly location. The
few remaining ones were now being tossed by the rising
wind against the fountain just visible at the corner of the
house, against Danny and Jamie running through the raindrops toward the kitchen entrance.

She glanced at the textbooks and grimaced. She wasn't
getting any studying done; she'd much rather spend the remaining time before the interview doing something that
would keep her mind occupied, that would keep her hands
occupied and that she would enjoy. Afterschool hot chocolate
with two lively adolescents was probably just the right prescription. Since Meg had heard the cook tell Mrs. Tompkins
she was leaving to do the week's shopping, she and the kids
would have that glorious kitchen to themselves.

Instead of going directly through the maid's pantry to the
kitchen, Meg took the door to the hallway and detoured
through a downstairs powder room where she gathered two
large towels for them to dry off.

She didn't see them when she first entered the kitchen, but
eventually spotted them in the alcove that housed the commercial refrigerator, bent over, examining the shelves for
something to eat. They were silent until Jamie straightened,
closed the door she had opened and stood tapping her foot
until Danny retrieved his snack and turned to face her.

"I'm not sorry," Danny said as he slammed his door.

"I know," Jamie told him. "And that's what's so sad
about this whole incident. You should be."

"Why? That guy's a total loser. He needed to be taught
a lesson."

Danny whirled around, and Meg caught her hand to her
mouth to stifle a cry. His lip was swollen and split, and blood
spattered his ripped shirt.

"Yes," Jamie said agreeably, "he did. But not necessarily
by you."

"Right." Danny saw Meg then. He paused a beat, but he
didn't speak to her as he marched to the work table and

plopped down the food he carried. "So who else was going to do it, Jamie? You? You were all for tucking our tails and slithering away. Where was all this fancy fighting stuff you're supposed to know?"

Then Jamie saw her. She nodded at her, gave her a reluctant little smile and turned back to Danny with determination in every inch of her reed-thin body. "That fancy fighting stuff, as you call it, is too important to waste on a thirteen-year-old bully who can be handled with words, or by simply ignoring him."

Meg sagged against the doorjamb as relief flooded her. A fight at school. A far cry from what she had thought when she first saw her son. A fight at school. *Oh, Danny.* Her disappointment moaned through her. *I thought you were doing so much better.*

"Like you were?"

"Yes. And we were almost home free until you decided to play hero."

"He grabbed you."

"And I was handling it."

"You were talking to him like he was somebody worth talking to instead of the scumbag he is. Guys like that don't listen to talk."

Jamie scooted her carton of yogurt onto the table and fisted her hands on her hips. "Not everybody is like your dad, Danny."

That caught him, and Meg, by surprise. "How—how do you know about my dad?"

"I heard my dad talking to Tully. About security. About what to do if your dad shows up in Avalon."

"Oh, great." Danny glared at his mother, and Meg saw the sense of betrayal in his eyes at her having shared what had always been their secret. "One, big, cops' reunion. Which one of them is going to hand me over to him?"

"Neither one," Jamie told him.

"Sure." Danny looked at the food but didn't move toward it, and then he looked at the girl who had been his best friend. "So tell me. How do you afford to live in this town? Small-town cops don't make that much money. Is your dad on the take?''

Meg gasped at the attack. She ought to stop this, now, before it got completely out of hand, but Jamie spoke before she found her voice.

"You're not going to make me fight with you, either," Jamie said with quiet dignity. "I'm proud of my father. He's here because this is where he wants to be, and because this is where I want to be. We may not have as much money as Edward Carlton, but we darn sure have enough to live in Avalon, and I'm real glad he's not off chasing people who blow up airplanes and bomb schools and…and kill little kids anymore. So if you want me to fight you, Danny, you meet me at the Department gym and we'll do it right, but don't you pick on me because you're scared."

"Scared?" Meg saw the flush that confirmed Jamie's soft attack. "You think I'm scared?"

"I think we're all scared sometimes. That's what my dad told me. And I know that when I'm scared, sometimes I act mad."

"Well, I'm not acting. I am mad," Danny rose up until his face was almost even with hers. "Good and mad. Not scared. Got that?"

Now Meg did have to speak. "Danny," she said softly.

He whirled to face her, and for a second, until Marianna joined her at the doorway, his expression lost some of its belligerence. "Mad," he repeated. "Just…mad." Then he grabbed his new blue windbreaker from the back of a nearby chair and ran from the room, back out into the rain.

Meg stepped forward to follow him but was stopped by Marianna's soft hand on her own. "Let him go. It's not that cold outside, and he'll be safe anywhere in Avalon."

Meg knew she was right, but Danny was hurting.

"He needs some time alone," Marianna said gently. "From the looks of him, he's already lost a fight today, and I'm sure he thinks he's too old for his mother to come chasing after him."

"I'm sorry, Ms. Wilson." Jamie said, shrugging in a combination of chagrin and disgust.

"For what?" Meg asked. "For being a very wise young woman?"

Jamie grimaced. "Apparently not wise enough. I meant to make him think, not drive him away."

"He needs to think, Jamie. Both of us needed to be reminded of that." She shook her head. She'd put it off too long, but now she was going to have to do something about Danny's increasingly hostile attitude and do it soon before he antagonized every potential friend here in Avalon. But first she had to put this surprisingly adult young woman at ease. "I came to make some hot chocolate. Would you—both of you—like to share a cup with me?"

Jamie grinned at her. "Sure. I almost never turn down hot chocolate. But aren't you busy?"

"No, I—" Or was she?

"I'm afraid you don't have time for that right now." Marianna took the forgotten towels from Meg's arm and placed them on the table. "Tommy asked me to find you. They're here."

With a brief apology to Jamie, Meg headed toward the study and the too-long-postponed interview with the FBI. Marianna walked with her as a silent but surprisingly comforting companion. The interview wouldn't be too bad, Meg knew. After all, she was the victim in this investigation. And Lucas would be there. He wouldn't let her be subjected to more than she could handle.

How easily she'd come to depend upon him. How easily she had almost destroyed his trust in her with her careless greed for affection. She stopped in an alcove just before they reached the main hall as Jamie's words, *all* of Jamie's words, played through her mind. It seemed her early impression of Lucas as a battle-scarred gladiator who had spent his life deflecting assaults and abuses and indignities from those who couldn't defend themselves had been closer to truth than fantasy. God help him, she would never begin to imagine the danger he must have put himself in.

"Meg?" Marianna asked softly, turning and walking back to where Meg had stopped.

"Did he?" Meg asked, needing to know.

"Did who?"

"Lucas. Did he do those things Jamie told Danny?"

Marianna hesitated, studying Meg. For a moment her eyes shuttered and she was more, much more than the quiet tasteful woman who had been so much help, and then she was Marianna again, tiny, delicate and sheltered. "Yes," she said, "he did."

Only one man waited with Lucas in the study. He turned from his conversation with Lucas as she entered the room alone, because Marianna had gently but firmly left her at the door.

"Ms. Wilson," he said, and she heard the same trace of the South in his voice as she heard in Lucas's. "I'm Trent Dawson. I'm delighted to meet you at last, and I'll work with you to make this interview as painless as possible."

As painless as possible wasn't completely painless, Meg learned as the afternoon progressed. But it could have been worse, much worse. Trent Dawson wanted memories, memories she didn't have. He wanted to solve a decades-old major case and he seemed to think she had the key to the puzzle.

"I don't remember," she said at last, staring out the window at the worsening rain. "I've been over this with Lucas and with Edward: I've looked at the pictures and the movies, and Edward has shared his memories with me, but I have none of my own. Don't you know I'd tell you if I had any? These people stole the lives of two people and changed the course of mine and my brother's. Don't you know I want them caught? Don't you know I want them punished? I just can't help you."

"Meg."

Lucas had moved to stand beside her at the window. She saw the concern in his eyes, and when she turned she saw the frustration in Trent Dawson's. "It's all right," she told Lucas. "I'm all right."

But it wasn't, and neither was she. Nothing about this situation was right, and she doubted if it ever would be.

"Would you be agreeable to hypnosis?"

"What good would that do?" Lucas asked.

None. Absolutely none. Meg knew that with a certainty. And maybe it was time these two men did too. "No."

She walked to her brother's desk and seated herself behind it, searching for comfort in the distance it put between her and the FBI agent, and in the memory of the power she had wielded from this position as she signed documents relating to literally millions of dollars.

"I've tried hypnosis," she said. When Lucas glanced sharply at her in surprise, she almost smiled. Almost. But the memory of those frustrating efforts was too grim for humor. "A woman I worked with a number of years ago was studying for her doctorate in psychology. I became a testing subject for her. Even then I recognized there were gaps in my early memories. The object of her project was to help me explore them."

"What happened?"

How like Lucas to know that something had happened. Something disturbing. Something that had left her hypnotist frustrated and Meg no more enlightened than before.

"I'm a good hypnotic subject," Meg said. "At least that's what she told me. I went easily into an altered state of consciousness, I responded well to questions, I experienced a vivid and complex set of sensory impressions. Up to—or rather back to—a point. Beyond that, I adamantly refused to go. If she pushed me to regress further, as she did in repeated sessions, I simply broke the trance."

Lucas stepped to her side and dropped his hand onto her shoulder. Meg glanced at it, tempted beyond all reason to reach up, to link her fingers with his, to hold on to him so that he would never let her go. Instead she leaned her head against the back of the chair, closed her eyes and relived a memory that made no more sense now than the first time she had recalled it.

"I was in my room at the Stemples. I'd had a nightmare—

we never were able to bring up any specific memories of that—and was crying. The room was dark. A man, an older man I think, but one I couldn't see, don't remember ever seeing, was trying to quiet me. The door opened from the hall, and a spear of light came into the room. That's how I identified the room. Audrey stood in the doorway and demanded that he—this unknown man—keep me quiet because they had company.''

"She didn't ask what was wrong with you or why you were crying?'' Lucas asked.

"Because they had company?'' Trent Dawson prompted. "Are you sure those were her words?''

"Not exactly.'' The words were now engraved in Meg's memory. They hadn't really surprised her when she'd dredged them up the first time because they were so representative of the way Audrey Stemple had always treated her. "She said…'' Some little vestige of shame must still linger, because Meg hesitated. She swallowed once, forcing back the shame. *She* wasn't the one who had been insensitive to the needs of a child. Why not tell them?

"She said, 'For God's sake, shut her up. There are people downstairs.'''

Lucas's hand tightened on her shoulder. This time Meg did lift her hand to cover his.

"And you remember nothing before that time?'' Dawson asked.

"Nothing.''

"And the older man in this memory, was he some sort of domestic servant or family friend?''

"I don't know,'' Meg said. "I just don't know.''

"Can you describe him?'' Lucas asked. "Can you remember anything else about him, Meg? Anything at all?''

Now Meg did smile. The awful loneliness of her childhood didn't have to be kept hidden any longer—couldn't be kept hidden any longer. And she had heard in Trent Dawson's voice the same outrage she had first heard in Lucas's. "I can do better than that. I can give you the name and address of my hypnotist.''

She looked up at Lucas. "I told you once I didn't want you to record our conversations because I wasn't comfortable not knowing who would listen to them. I don't want the world to listen, but I don't think I would mind you hearing these. You see, she taped all our sessions, and unless she's changed completely in the past four years, she'll still have the tapes, all neatly dated and labeled."

Lucas walked Trent as far as the agent's car parked under the porte cochere. "Why would anyone so ill adapted for parenting adopt a child?"

Trent paused with one hand on the open door. "To cement a faltering marriage, to promote political ambition, to gain status in the family or community. And those are the least harmful ones. At least it doesn't seem the Stemples had any of the truly dark reasons. Their abuse doesn't appear to have been physical."

"Right. They just took a little girl who'd been loved and treasured, who had gone through only God knows what kind of trauma, and proceeded to convince her she was worthless."

"We might want to try hypnosis again. Depending on what you learn from Meg's tapes," Trent said.

"You know I'll turn any pertinent information over to you immediately. The rest will be up to Meg."

Lucas didn't like the knowing look in his friend's eyes as he absorbed that quick response. Or the half smile that lingered. "It's like that, is it?" Trent asked.

He elected not to answer that question. "You might like to know that Paul Slater, Carlton's P.I., hasn't been able to find anything on the alleged niece who was reported by the Stemples to have been Meg's birth mother—or have they given up on that story by now? He did learn that the office of the attorney who handled the adoption mysteriously burned shortly before the attorney caught a plane to Brazil only one step ahead of the tax boys."

"It's driving you crazy, isn't it?" Trent asked. "Having

to rely on Paul Slater and me for information you want to be out there gathering?''

"I'm needed here.''

"Yes. But what about what you need? The Bureau would take you in a minute, Lucas. You know that. You wouldn't have to go back into covert work.''

"My friend.'' Lucas clapped his hand on Trent's shoulder and pushed down, urging him into the car. "Please stop trying to fix my life. I know what I need to do, and I know what I want to do.''

"But are you doing it?''

"Go,'' Lucas said, smiling but feeling little humor. "Solve this case. Make your career and take the glory. Believe me, I don't want either one.''

Yes, Lucas thought as he watched Trent's car vanish through the driveway gates. He knew what he needed to do. And he knew what he wanted to do. Unfortunately, they weren't the same thing.

He wanted Meg. In his life. Smiling at him in that wistful little way that told him how much she wanted him in hers. Touching him with her healing, graceful fingers. Standing beside him with her stubborn little chin thrust out as they faced the problems life was sure to throw at them. Loving him with an uninhibited, unselfish passion he had never dreamed could be his.

What he needed to do was distance himself from her, turn her safety over to Tully and back away before she completed convincing herself that she felt something for him. What he needed to do was get out of her life and get on with the business of redeeming his own. But he could no more do that than he could seize the glimpse of heaven she so unwittingly offered him.

You'll take care of her? Edward, who commanded companies but who found it almost impossible to ask for anything for himself, had asked this of him, and Lucas, who counted Edward as one of his few true friends had answered, *Yes. Yes, of course.*

A slash of rain found its way under the portico and raked at his cheek. Lucas lifted his hand to it. The tiny wound Meg had inflicted had already healed, but the reason for it might never heal. He had pushed her too hard, too far and too fast into a realm she hadn't wanted to visit. That was a mistake he wouldn't make again, and one he wouldn't let anyone else make with her.

He caught a glimpse of something blue in the swirling rain and glanced toward it. Danny stood in the shelter of a towering fir just beside the drive, but still, he was drenched—drenched and defiant and radiating anger. Or maybe fear. Sometimes those two were hard to separate.

Lucas met the boy's steady glare with appraisal as he noted the too-visible signs of the recent fight at school he'd already learned about. He could order the boy into the house—fat lot of good that would do. He could run him down and drag him in. He could ignore him. None of those seemed like viable choices. Meg's son had been through too much in his young life, but hauling that brand-new chip around on his shoulder wasn't going to make the rest of his life any easier. At least he still had a life.

Lucas tried to imagine what would have gotten through to him at twelve. Probably nothing. But then, no one had tried.

"I'm not your enemy."

"Yeah. Tell it to someone who cares."

"I just did." Lucas took a step toward the door, away from the boy, who looked as though he might bolt at any perceived threat. "You have a mother who loves you and a family that welcomed you. That's not going to change regardless of what you do. But you have friends you haven't met yet and opportunities you probably never even thought of just waiting for you. Don't throw those away because they weren't there for you last week or last month—they're here now."

"And what are you going to do? Make me meet those friends? Make me figure out what those opportunities are? Make me choose the ones you want me to?"

No. Lucas wouldn't. But someone in Danny's young life

would have done that. He'd like to have Wilson alone for half an hour. Instead, he shook his head. "What I'm going to do is go into the house and get out of this rain. You can, too, if you want."

Had he done the right thing? he wondered as he entered the house. Boys' egos were such fragile things, battered as they were by hormones and pride. Danny's must be especially fragile now, after his having to be so mature and so street smart for so long.

He'd almost reached the front hall when he heard the outside door open and close quietly behind him and the sound of wet athletic shoes on the polished floor. Lucas smiled to himself but gave no indication that he had heard Danny's surreptitious entry.

Now he just had one more confrontation before he could take his own hormones and pride and get out of this house before they caused him to take a step that neither he nor Meg needed to take.

Meg had returned to the window where she had taken up sentry duty earlier. She didn't hear him when he entered the study. She did hear him when he closed the door behind him and leaned against it. She dropped the sheer curtain she had pulled to one side of the window and turned. In the first second her eyes betrayed her, telling him how much she had wanted him to return. In the next she shuttered them as quickly as she had dropped the curtain over the window.

"Is Trent gone?" she asked.

"Yes."

"Will he be back?"

"Probably."

Her shoulders sagged before she rallied. "Thank you for being here."

What could he say to that? *It was my pleasure? It was my job? I'd be anywhere you needed me?* "You did fine."

"Oh, yeah. Right."

"I'm not any good for you." Where had that come from? He couldn't call back his words, but he would have given half of his benighted life to do so when he saw her eyes darken as if she had been struck. "Meg, I—"

Up went her chin. "I believe you've misread the situation, Sheriff," she said, and if he hadn't already seen her pull this valiant act too many times, he might have been convinced. "I've been taking care of myself for most of my life, and while I appreciate the help you've given me, and I hope you will continue to give me in your official capacity, I assure you that's all I...that's all I expect from you."

Nicely said, Meg, he thought. So nicely said that someone else might have believed it. Maybe even she believed it. But even if that was all she expected from him, it wasn't all she wanted or needed. And he couldn't distance himself from her without proving to her that her needs meant nothing. God, had anyone ever cared about Meg's needs?

Or her pride?

Because he knew that if he wasn't careful, he could shatter the dignity she had so tightly wrapped around herself.

"I'm sorry," he said. "Apparently I was out of line."

Meg's lips quirked in a wry grin. Obviously she wasn't sure whether to believe his words, but caught in her own trap she knew she had to act as though she did.

And that was just fine. At least that way he could continue to act as though *he* believed them. At least for now. Because without that, he would be distanced from her, and he knew now that was the last thing Meg needed. She needed him near her. And if he was careful to make sure that she didn't make more of this dependency than was truly necessary to get her through the next few weeks, then maybe neither one of them would get hurt too badly.

Eight

Meg knew by now that no family member was ever left completely alone in her brother's huge old house, but she certainly felt as though she had been. She sat in a corner of the love seat with her bare feet tucked up beneath her and her chin propped on her knees, enjoying a cozy fire in her sitting room and nursing a second cup of hot chocolate. Even though it was a bright, clear Saturday morning, she was still in her nightgown, loath to start any of the many projects that had so insidiously filled the once-endless emptiness of her new life.

Danny, with the exuberance and excitement that had always been his trademark, had gone off with Mrs. Tompkins to visit her nephew at his family's ranch.

For some reason Marianna had not shown up for her almost-daily visit, and her absence showed Meg just how much she had grown to count on the woman's gentle presence.

Meg wanted Edward to come home, wanted to explore more of the closeness she had felt with him the one evening they had spent together, wanted to develop the growing sense of family she felt with him during their too-limited telephone calls. But Jennie was in precarious health, and Meg wouldn't have him leave her, wouldn't have him jeopardize what she had seen and felt between him and his new wife.

And Lucas—Lucas had returned from Florida, from listening to the tapes and visiting the one friend she'd trusted enough to open up to about her past, the one person she'd trusted to see to her son's safety in their Plan B. But he wouldn't come today. Not without a serious reason. Not without someone else present to act as a buffer between them. Not after that fiasco Monday when she had told him all she expected of him was...was nothing.

For days after that afternoon at Lucas's house, Meg had cringed whenever she thought of her actions. She might still be doing so if it hadn't been for his unexpected words, *I'm not any good for you.*

She'd reacted out of hurt pride when she'd told him she expected nothing more from him than help in his official capacity. Not that it wasn't the truth; she didn't expect more. But she could hope for more, a lot more.

And she hadn't been the only one trying to save face in that stilted conversation, because she hadn't been the only one who had exposed needs then or in his basement.

Why hadn't she seen that sooner? Or had she, and just not been willing to acknowledge that despite his obvious strength, Lucas Lambert was as needy, as hungry, as *lonely* as she was, and he was as determined as she was to hide his need, his hunger and his loneliness. Imagine that.

She'd thought once that he looked like someone who had spent his life deflecting assaults and indignities away from those who couldn't defend themselves and taking them on himself if necessary. Now she knew what he was, even if he'd never admit it to her: a modern day gladiator, but with something more deadly serious than games taking him into battle. And she now recognized battle scars that not even his civilized veneer of expensive tailoring could hide from someone who really looked. And now she more than suspected that Lucas had never been cherished, either.

She just didn't know how to convince him that she was someone who would cherish him.

Or if he would let her.

When she heard the light tap on her door, the last person she expected to enter was Jamie, looking vaguely uneasy but completely determined. "I told the substitute dragon on door duty that you wouldn't mind if I came in. Do you?"

Meg set her cup on the side table and gestured toward the adjacent chair. "Of course not. I thought you'd be with Danny."

Jamie grimaced. "Yeah. Well, I thought it might be kind of neat for him to do 'guy' things today. Besides—I've got this father-daughter dinner at school next month. I wonder...would you, I mean, I know I don't have any— Well, heck. Would you go shopping with me? Would you help me pick out something to wear?"

"Yes. I'd love to. But what about Marianna? She's great at things like that."

Jamie scooted across the room and folded herself into the chair. "Yes. She is. For you and Jennie and I don't know how many others. She can look at you and see just exactly what would be right for you, but I'm afraid that when Aunt Marianna looks at me, all she sees is this scrawny little baby in a crib. And I guess I would ask her, anyway, because I wouldn't want to hurt her feelings, but she's not feeling too good today. We like to let her rest when she's not feeling well. Otherwise, she'd just keep going and going and going."

Going and going and going—kind of like Jamie with the information that dropped from her so heedlessly. Meg didn't know whether to laugh in sheer enjoyment of the girl's company, commiserate with her or be concerned over Marianna's hitherto undisclosed health problem or question her previously unknown status as a member of Jamie's family.

"Why don't you find a cup of hot chocolate in the kitchen," she said instead. "I'll dress and be down in fifteen minutes."

Jamie looked dubious at the time schedule, but Meg surprised Jamie and herself by walking through the kitchen door exactly sixteen minutes later.

"Where did you want to do this shopping? I'm afraid the only car I'd feel comfortable taking is gone right now."

"That's okay. There are a couple of really neat places in town close enough for us to walk."

"Walk?" It seemed forever since she had been allowed that simple pleasure. Meg shrugged. "Why not?"

"Great." Jamie set her cup down and snatched up a scarlet-colored, down-filled jacket. "And if anybody asks about Jennie, and somebody's bound to because they love her in this town, you know, just tell them she's doing fine and that Reverend Winthrop will keep everybody posted. Okay?"

If *anybody* asked about Jennie? It seemed that walking with Jamie didn't give Meg the protection from questions that being with Lucas did. Almost everybody asked about Jennie, about Edward, about her.

"They're not malicious," Jamie told her after the fourth person stopped them on the sidewalk. "Just curious. And almost everybody thought Dad and Jennie were going to be an item—he was her guardian, you know—until Edward found her, so it's only natural..."

Meg let Jamie's words pass without comment, but endless thoughts buzzed through her mind. *An item? Lucas and Jennie? Her guardian?* Yes. Jennie was tiny and delicate and exactly the kind of person who looked as though she'd need Lucas's protection. Why wouldn't he be taken with her?

Jamie shrugged and slanted a glance at Meg. Why? Hoping she hadn't heard? "Dad won't let me date yet," she continued valiantly. "I'll bet you had a lot of boyfriends when you were my age, could you maybe..."

Now Meg shrugged. Sure she had. *All arms and legs and knees and elbows and so hungry for affection...* She steered her thoughts away from that direction as she steered Jamie away from the ice cream parlor toward a promising-looking boutique. "You'd lose your bet," she said.

"Really?" Jamie stopped in the middle of the sidewalk and turned to look at her. "I mean, you're so...so *together.*

I thought for sure you must have always been that way. Sometimes I feel so klutzy. I guess, when I look at you, I feel kind of hopeful that one day I'll be as confident and as, as...

Meg reached for Jamie's hand to stop its vague gesturing. "Jamie. If I'd had only a portion of your confidence and your poise at your age, I would own half the world by now. Trust me."

Jamie giggled. It was a surprisingly girlish sound and one which shattered the intensity of the moment. "Don't look now, Meg," she said conspiratorially, "but I think you do."

They found the perfect dress in the second shop they visited. It was on the sale rack, to which Meg naturally gravitated. Jamie eyed it suspiciously when Meg held it out for her, but all suspicion had fled when she stepped from the dressing room minutes later, draped in innocence and provocation, sophistication and charm that delicately emphasized her long bones and fine features.

"Oh," Jamie whispered. "Dad is going to be so proud of me."

And he would be. Meg fought back an irrational jealousy. Had James Stemple ever been proud of her? How long had it been since she had stopped even hoping he would be? Jamie was one lucky girl. She caught the eye of the hovering salesclerk and nodded. "Do you have shoes?" she asked Jamie. "A purse? A slinky slip?"

Jamie left her packages stowed in Meg's closet, not willing to risk transporting them on the bicycle that usually served her so well, or to risk letting her father in on the surprise he was due by revealing her purchases too soon, Meg suspected.

"That was fun," Jamie told her as she prepared to leave. "Can we, maybe, do it again some time? You know, like the fellows have their guy stuff, could we...maybe..."

"Do girl things?" Meg finished for her.

"Yes." Jamie opened the front door and stood half in, half out of the foyer. "I mean, I know you probably have all sorts of important stuff you have to do, but—"

"Jamie." Meg silenced the girl's stammering. "I have

never had anyone to do girl things with. I would be honored—''

"You would? Great." Jamie leaned forward and gave Meg a quick hug before she stepped onto the front porch. "I promise I won't be a pest," she called as she closed the door behind her.

"Girl stuff." Meg shook her head and turned to go back upstairs. Mrs. Tompkins stood in the hallway, immaculate as usual, but wearing not-so-usual jeans, boots and a Western shirt. "How was your visit?" Meg asked her. "Or maybe a better question would be, how was Danny during your visit?"

"It was…interesting," Mrs. Tompkins admitted, obviously bypassing the second part of Meg's question. "If you don't mind, I'd like to take him back out there tomorrow after church."

"He enjoyed the visit, then? He got along with your nephew? He wasn't too much trouble?"

Mrs. Tompkins didn't quite answer that question. "He made a new friend today, or tried to—a yellow hound named Skeeter that's even more wary of new friends than Danny is—but he probably hasn't finished putting together all the parallels. He will though, in time. He's a good boy, Mrs. Wilson. Never doubt that."

Meg hadn't; but once she had realized that his attitude wasn't improving with time, she simply hadn't known how to reach him. But if a ranch, a boy his age, a housekeeper who was a martial arts expert and a stray dog could reach him, she'd give all of them her blessings.

"Where is he?"

With a wry chuckle Mrs. Tompkins nodded toward the stairs to the game room. "Where else? Fighting off alien invaders."

All right. Meg felt confident today, and lucky, and happy to be here and safe with her son. Maybe she would help fight those invaders. At one time she and Danny had been a pretty formidable team at video games and in life. "Do you suppose…" And this was kind of nice, too, although she might never get used to it. "Do you suppose you could find us a snack or a late lunch and bring it downstairs?"

The house wasn't completely dark. Lucas had seen a light in the upstairs room he knew was Meg's, as well as a few scattered through the downstairs rooms. Tommy was awake; he'd called her from the office and she'd had the gates open for him, just as she had the door open when he stepped up on the porch.

"Meg is upstairs," she said when he entered the foyer. "I didn't see any point in upsetting her before it was absolutely necessary. Go on into the study. I'll ask her to come down."

Lucas nodded. In Edward's study he found that Tommy had already been there, to light the lamps and feed the glowing fire.

He hadn't wanted to bother Meg before it was absolutely necessary, either. And maybe it wasn't. Maybe he could have waited until the morning. Or maybe he could have just telephoned as he had phoned Edward as soon as Paul Slater had called him. But telephoning Meg would have been the coward's way. As waiting until morning to tell her would have been.

Meg swept into the study, magnificent in a long, dark-garnet-colored velvet robe hastily tied over a long, frothy white confection. Apparently she'd hurried downstairs when Tommy announced he was there, because her face was free of makeup and her wet hair was slicked back. For a moment she reminded him of that vulnerable young woman she had seemed when he first met her. For a moment he allowed himself the fantasy of thinking she had run to his side because that was where she wanted to be, but only until he saw the anxiety that momentarily darkened her eyes.

"What's wrong?"

No. She knew him too well to think he would come from no more than a need to see her at this time of the night— that he would come from no more than a need to see her at any time.

She stopped just inside the door, and a brief glance at her

revealed none of her tension. But her hands did. Oh, those give-away hands. To all but the most casual observer they would appear clasped loosely in front of her. But again, as in the Tulsa interrogation room a lifetime before, they trembled with the energy she exerted not to clench them.

Lucas crossed the room and took those revealing hands in his. She looked at him, startled, but he shook his head and led her across the room to a wing chair in front of the fire. She wouldn't sit. Instead, when he realized he still held her hands captive and protected, and released her, she walked to the fireplace and whirled to face him.

"What's wrong?" she repeated.

She almost had it right. Apparently she'd had Marianna give her lessons on imperiousness along with those on family history. There was only a slight quiver to her stubborn chin, only a slight quaver in her soft voice, only a slight shadow of uncertainty in her expressive eyes.

She almost had it right, and he couldn't destroy her confidence by letting her know he saw through her bravado to a little girl crying in the dark only to be told to shut up. He could, however, keep her from having to face alone the threat of someone else exposing her insecurity.

"The California people have located you."

Meg's expression froze, and for a slow count of three she straightened to an almost unbearably upright posture. Then with a wry, humorless laugh, she released the visible tension and all attempts at bravado. She looked at him with the weight of years of rejection in her eyes.

"That you're here at this time of night tells me they've done more than locate me. Who's coming? And when do they arrive?"

"Blake, James and Audrey." He saw each name hit her like a blow, but she lifted her chin and looked at him steadily, waiting for the rest. "Paul Slater's operative followed them to a private airport where they chartered a plane. Their pilot filed a flight plan for Avalon. I'm on my way to the airport now to meet them."

"And so the protestations of familial love begin."

Why didn't she get mad, throw something, yell? She was entitled to. Didn't she know that? "Not necessarily," he told her. "Not unless you let them."

She closed her eyes briefly before meeting his. "I've never been strong enough to face them down, or coward enough to let someone else do it for me. I don't suppose I am now, either."

"It isn't cowardice to rely on someone else's greater strength, Meg."

"It isn't?" She shook her head, clearly not believing his words, but she didn't pursue that argument. "Together? They're arriving together? I can't believe they've resolved their differences."

Neither could Lucas, especially after listening to hours of taped recordings of Meg's hypnotically induced memories that had told far more than Meg had willingly revealed to him about the bleakness of her childhood and her marriage. He hadn't talked to her about the tapes yet; he wasn't sure if he could without revealing to her the rage he felt when he thought of the life she had endured. And his rage wasn't what she needed to feel—not until she had admitted and purged some of her own.

"How much time do we have?" Meg ran her fingers through her still-damp hair and grimaced. "I'll need a few minutes."

"For what?" Lucas asked, although he had a nasty suspicion he knew the answer.

She had already started from the room. Now she stopped and turned. "I can't meet them like this." She attempted a smile, that, like her earlier bravado, almost made it. "Marianna would have my hide."

She'd never been strong enough to face them down, had she? And yet that was exactly what she intended to do tonight. At that moment Lucas's pride in the surprising contradiction that was Meg Carlton swelled to still another new height.

"You don't have to do this."

"Don't I?" Meg asked. "I'm afraid I do. I can't let them

chase me into hiding again. If I do, I'll never have my life—
I started to say 'back' but that isn't right, is it? I've never
had it. No. I want to see them now and get this over with.
Waiting won't help.''

"Yes. It will.'' He saw a glimmer of hope in Meg's eyes,
but it quickly faded to be replaced by determination he knew
he had to deflect. "In this case, it certainly will help. They
want something from you, something each of them is willing
to band together with a former antagonist to obtain. I'm
sorry, but you and I both know what it probably is. Wishing
they were different won't make it so, and it won't erase the
past. So let them come to you, Meg, in more ways than just
by air. Let them be the supplicants. Let them seek an audience. It's within your power now to make them sweat, to
make them consider and rehearse and dwell on their reasons
for coming. I think you owe it to yourself, at least this once,
to be the one in power.''

"Power?'' Meg asked, fisting her hands and raising them
unconsciously and futilely. "Do you think I'll ever really
have any kind of power over people who've demonstrated
time after time, my whole life, their power over me?''

He took the three steps that separated them and caught her
shoulders in his hands, stilling her actions and stilling her
words. She tilted her head the slight distance necessary to
look into his eyes, searching for answers he knew he
shouldn't give her. He saw the moment she took his reticence
for rejection and tried to pull away from him. He didn't let
her go.

"What's this for?'' she asked finally, with an attempt at
the bravado that had carried her so well for so long. "To
give me courage to face the troops?''

"No.'' Lucas drew her closer. She came willingly, but
doubts again shadowed her eyes. In an innocent, provocative
movement, she moistened her lips. "No,'' he repeated, hearing the rasp in his voice, knowing that at that moment he
wanted nothing more than to take the invitation she so un-
knowingly offered him, to bend the short distance that sep-

arated them and taste again the heaven of her kiss, to feel again the welcome of her arms.

"No," he said again as he began distancing himself from her and from all he couldn't take. "It's to give me courage to leave you alone here tonight while I go face the troops."

Meg drove the car the cook usually used, a late-model, unobtrusive minivan—something that she as Meg Wilson would never have been able to afford, but so functional that had she been raised Meg Carlton she would probably never have considered driving. It was a good choice, she thought— putting her squarely in the middle of two lives, neither one of which was fully hers.

Mrs. Tompkins had tried to persuade her to wait at the house, but in this Meg had been insistent.

She'd had to come.

Did Lucas Lambert really think that once she had seen the naked emotion and need in his eyes she would let him go off and fight her battles alone for her? Too many people had already done that to him; she wouldn't be another that used and discarded him. She wouldn't be another that turned away from him after he'd seen her through crisis and disaster.

Hogwash! The doubt had crept into her mind as she'd hurried to dress and follow Lucas to the airport. Sheer, un-adulterated pig shampoo! No one except Danny had ever needed her—not in her entire lifetime—so what made her think Lucas did?

Maybe the way he held her. Maybe the way he *didn't* touch her. Maybe the regret she'd also glimpsed in his eyes.

And maybe she was living in a fairy tale—a fairy tale all in her mind. Some Cinderella she made. Instead of balls and happily ever after she was closeted with lawyers and trust agreements. At five ten, she was much too tall to have feet small enough to fit into any glass slipper. And if Jamie's unwitting comments were to be believed, the one prince she wanted was either still in love with or just getting over an-other princess—a real one.

All right. Maybe he didn't want her, Meg Wilson. She

swallowed that knowledge like the bitter pill it was, that it had always been, but that didn't mean she couldn't give something to him, at least support while he fought her battles, at least the knowledge that she appreciated what he did for her.

She didn't have to let him know how important he'd become to her, how empty her life would be once he left it, or how she would give almost anything, certainly at least the Carlton money which she wasn't sure she was entitled to, anyway, to have him want her to be a part of his life.

The airport runway lights came on just as she pulled off the road into the parking lot. A cluster of cars waited there: Lucas's as well as two other deputies' vehicles, those that probably belonged to the airport management and security, and Norris Huxtable's van from the lodge. She parked at the end of the row of vehicles and slipped out of her minivan.

She'd dressed all in black, in the same softly tailored wool slacks and cowl-collared, mohair sweater she'd worn for her shopping trip with Jamie, but this time she'd added a quick application of the dramatic makeup Marianna had insisted she learn to apply, dangerously high-heeled boots, because, as Marianna had told her, *one never knows when a little intimidation will come in handy,* a soft, black felt fedora, and a black cape for which she was eminently grateful in the increasingly windy and rapidly chilling night air.

From overhead she heard the drone of an approaching plane. She knew where Lucas would be—on the runway side of the chrome, glass and black marble art deco terminal she now faced. The sidewalk forked in front of her. One path led to the well-lit entrance; the other, illuminated now with only a few scattered security lights, toward a cluster of hangars to the north. Meg moved into the shadow and toward the hangars.

She heard the low murmur of men's voices as she rounded the first hangar and stopped at the gate in the chain link fence that separated her from the runway. Avalon's airport had a state-of-the-art departure ramp; she had used it the day she'd arrived on Edward's jet. The new visitors, however, were to be shown something quainter. Meg felt her lips quirk. Her uninvited visitors were not being given a dignitary's welcome.

Lucas stood to the back of the group of men at the arrival gate, but obviously in command. Meg let herself watch his strength and calm with unguarded admiration and a wistful longing she refused to give in to—she was here for him, not herself—as he conferred quietly with Tully, who held a cellular telephone or radio, relaying information to Lucas.

When Tully lowered the phone, Lucas looked directly toward where Meg stood hidden in the shadows, and she could have sworn he saw her there as he nodded. Probably not, she thought. If he had seen her he might have tried to send her away, for her own safety, of course—for her own peace of mind. Instead he turned his attention to the lights of the plane now circling the field.

Meg stepped deeper into the shadows of the hangar as a sleek twin-engine propeller driven plane made a graceful touchdown at the end of the landing strip and taxied toward the terminal. Although not so fine as Edward's jet, it was obviously a luxury airplane, and she wondered at the expense. James Stemple had always guarded his dollars, at least where she had been concerned. Had his investment portfolio and Blake's salary as a police detective grown to the point where they could afford such luxuries? Of course, she thought, foolish her, they probably considered this an investment, not an expense.

Two members of the airport staff pushed the ancient steel-grated ramp out to the side of the plane as the propellers slowed and stopped. A door in the side opened, and a uniformed steward stepped into view.

James was the first out. He still seemed taller than life, and more distinguished than even the minister at the oh-so-serious and dignified church to which they had paraded her every Sunday. In the glare of the lights, she saw that his hair was totally white now, silver, not gray, but that seemed to be the only sign of age he bore. And she also saw that he was not pleased by the sheriff's department and airport security uniforms he observed in the less-than-welcoming committee.

He glared at the ramp, not wide enough for two, said something over his shoulder to the person behind him in the plane and proceeded down the ramp with military precision.

Audrey followed him. The wind tormented her hair and her skirt, and she fought to control them before giving up the fight and holding on to the metal rail of the ramp as her glance darted from face to face in the small throng waiting below.

And then—then Blake stepped from the plane. Even knowing there was no way he could see her, Meg shrank back against the hangar wall. Funny. She'd thought he was taller than that. He'd always seemed so. And trimmer. Now he just looked like a well-dressed but slightly soft executive approaching his middle years. Only two years ago he'd still looked like the star quarterback of the high school football team who had won her heart and her hand before deciding he really didn't want either. Two years...

Danny's safe, she thought. *He'll never be able to hurt him again.* And for the first time, Meg truly understood the power of the Carlton wealth. She stood a little straighter in the shadows. Blake's words could hurt, his actions could wound Danny's fragile ego, but she had the power to prevent him from ever again getting close enough to physically harm her son.

Meg caught her hands to her mouth. Had she really not known that before? Had she only given lip service to understanding the words she'd spoken, the documents she'd signed and the promises Lucas and Edward and Fallon's legal staff had made? Maybe so, she realized. Maybe so. But she understood it now, and understanding gave her the courage to push forward, out of the shadows.

Nine

Meg wouldn't like knowing she'd been under surveillance since the moment she'd left her brother's house. Lucas cast one more quick glance toward the hangar. She wouldn't like knowing that he hoped to hell she stayed hidden in the shadows of the hangar. No matter what she thought of herself, Meg Carlton was no coward. She didn't have to prove that to him; he hoped she didn't choose tonight to prove it to herself.

James Stemple reached the bottom of the ramp and stood to one side to wait for his wife. He was distinguished looking and handsome in a public-relation image builder's sort of way; she was by anyone's standards an extremely attractive and well-turned-out woman of comfortable but not impressive wealth. They didn't look like monsters; but then, if monsters looked like monsters, they'd all be locked away.

Wilson was another matter. Or maybe it was just Lucas's lack of objectivity getting in the way. Blake wasn't a particularly tall man—he'd have to look up to Lucas, an advantage which Lucas fully intended to use—but he was stocky with

the thick neck and overly bulked shoulders of a weight lifter.
A weight lifter who'd stopped working out some time ago
and had more than begun the long slide into softness. Lucas
gave him one more scathing glance before nodding toward
Norris.

Norris Huxtable, with his BBC accent and his impeccable
tweed and leather country gentleman's hunting jacket,
stepped forward. "The Lodge's shuttle is waiting. If you'll
follow me, the ground crew will see to your luggage."

Audrey grasped her husband's arm and looked up in
alarm. "Oh, no. We're going to stay—"

"At the Lodge," Huxtable told her. "Those are the only
facilities available."

Blake pushed his way past Audrey. "You don't understand. We're here to visit family."

With a quick, wry grin at him, Tully stepped to one side,
and a path opened between Lucas and Avalon's unwelcome
visitors. He caught a glimpse of the quick conference between pilot and steward at the opened doorway above them
and knew that the tower had relayed the information that
their passengers might not be staying. He stopped a few feet
from the small cluster of intruders, ignoring Blake's bluster
and Audrey's nervous plucking of her husband's sleeve, and
speaking directly to James.

"No," Lucas said. "*You* don't understand. Avalon has no
public transportation, no rental cars are available and the only
lodging option you have is the one that you've just been
given."

With patient detachment, he watched James Stemple's
quick computation of the cost of his suit, his boots, his hair-
cut and his watch. Apparently he considered it sufficient to
merit his deigning to recognize him.

"You seem to be in a position of misplaced authority,
Mr.—"

"Lambert," Lucas told him, "Sheriff Lambert. And believe me, my authority is exactly where it needs to be."

He saw Blake's attempt at a conspiratorial grin as he thrust
his hand toward Lucas. "Sheriff? How convenient. I was

going to look you up tomorrow. I'm Blake Wilson, Detective Captain Wilson of the Simonville, California, PD.''

Lucas ignored the hand. "I know who you are and why you are here. I know that you were not invited by any resident of my county, that you did not bother to announce your intention to visit and that you have no legitimate business to transact within my jurisdiction. I know that it's late and that if you wish to rest before you return to Simonville, you should avail yourself of Mr. Huxtable's kind offer of transportation.''

Audrey turned toward him with a look of anguish he might have believed had he not known Meg, had he not heard her halting story of her childhood and her hypnotically recalled memories. "But I've come to see my daughter," she said. "My little girl. And my grandson. Surely you can't mean to keep me from them.''

"Want to bet I'll see more familial love in the next few weeks than I've seen in my entire life?''

For a moment he heard Meg's soft, dispirited words in his mind. But these words weren't dispirited, and while soft and quietly spoken, for his hearing only, they were audible. He heard Audrey gasp before he looked to his side. Meg stood there, looking like a dark, avenging angel.

"You have no daughter," Meg said with absolutely no emotion. "And you have had twelve years in which you have made no effort to see the boy you are now so eager to claim. Get back in the airplane or get in the van. The choice is yours, and it's more than you deserve.''

Stunned silence followed her words, until, with an almost visible click, Audrey remembered her role. "Margaret!" Audrey cried on a broken sob, but Meg swirled her cape around her and walked quietly and deliberately back into the shadows. Audrey threw off James's restraining hand and started after Meg only to be stopped by a wall of men—deputies, airport personnel and even Norris Huxtable's driver.

"This is—this is feudal," James said.

Lucas smiled at him. "This is Avalon. Tully?''

Tully stepped to his side. "Yes, sir.''

"Take over."

His first deputy's grin was one he reserved for special occasions, unholy and feral. Anyone who knew Tully Wilbanks knew there wasn't a malicious bone in his body. Their intruders didn't know him. Without another word, Lucas turned and walked away.

"Wait a minute!" he heard Blake bluster.

"Now it's this way," Tully told them as the wall of staff and friends kept the three at the edge of the tarmac while Lucas followed Meg into the shadows. "The airport has overnight accommodations for flight crews, so your pilot and his crew can stay here if that's what they want to do. But we've got ordinances that prohibit anyone from just setting up camp in the terminal—the vagrant problem, you know—and we'd sure hate to have to run you in. So what's it going to be, folks? Huxtable's digs are pretty spiffy. Presidents, kings and rock stars have stayed there, most of them more than once. Or we can have you fueled up and out of here within the hour."

He found Meg at the edge of the parking lot, trapped in a pool of light from a nearby security lamp, but blindly thrusting a key at the lock on Carlton's household staff's minivan. She jumped when he closed his hand over hers and guided the key to the lock, then pulled away and let him finish the task of unlocking the car. He dropped the keys onto the seat and closed the door before turning and taking her shoulders in his hands.

"You were magnificent," he said, and realized that was the second time that night he had applied that description to her.

She sniffed once before looking at him with tear-washed eyes. "I was a sniveling coward. I didn't say half of what I meant to."

He smiled at her. "More would have been overkill. They're still reeling from the shock of seeing you standing there."

He saw the first tear spill from her eyes. "I thought I could do it," she said brokenly. "I really thought I could face them and not feel anything. But I couldn't. All I wanted to know, all I wanted to ask was, *Why couldn't you love me?*"

"And someone should ask them that, Meg. But not you. You shouldn't have to be the one."

"Then who?" She sniffed again and attempted to swipe at her cheeks, but her hands were caught by her cape and his hands on her shoulders. "You? That's beyond even the scope of your very generous job description, Sheriff."

He couldn't help it. Would he be damned for taking this much, for telling himself it was for her need as much as it was for his? He pulled her closer to him. "And is it beyond the scope of what I, as a man, just a man, Megan, want to do for you?"

She tilted her head back, to look from beneath the hat brim. He caught it with one hand and pulled it from her, freeing her soft curls to the breeze. She had to see the need in his eyes, and for this moment he had to let her see it.

"Don't do this, Lucas," she pleaded softly. "Please don't do this to me again."

"Do what?" he asked.

"Don't let me think you want me. Don't let me think you care."

Why couldn't you love me?

Meg's words of a moment ago hung in the night air, paired forever with the ones she had just spoken, chilling him as all the reasons why he shouldn't, *couldn't,* love this woman, spewed from the dark sewers of his mind. He threw his head back, closing his eyes, but he couldn't let go of her. He surrendered her hat to the wind and once again grasped both her shoulders, holding her still, holding her near.

He felt the shudder that racked her, felt the ramrod stiffness of her posture as she drew in on herself, but it did no good, for him or for her. When he opened his eyes, he saw that hers brimmed with tears and rejection.

"See," she said in the same small voice he had heard too often on her tapes. "Even with the money and the education,

and all the artifice Marianna has taught me, I'm still not
someone that you, that anyone…could love.''

Now her eyes closed, in a futile attempt to hide her pain.

Not love her? How could anyone not love this fragile,
tenacious, artless, complicated woman?

How could he not love her?

Oh, God. How could he let himself love her?

With a strangled sob, she pushed away from him and fumbled for the car door. And he couldn't let her go. God help
him, he couldn't let her go.

He twisted her around and pulled her against his chest.

''Don't do this, Lucas,'' she moaned. ''Please don't do
this.''

She might as well tell him not to breathe as to tell him
not to hold her; at that moment, both were necessary for his
survival. He released her shoulders and caught her face in
his hands. ''Meg.'' Her name was a whispered plea, for ab-
solution, for solace, for the love that he'd needed as long as
she had and even now couldn't claim. He felt her breath,
sweet and warm on his cheek, felt the moment the tension
left her and she moved the step that had separated them,
heard her moan of surrender…heard the roar of powerful
twin engines start up, shattering the silence of the night. The
tension was back, in both of them, as they listened, as the
plane began moving. Familiar with the airport, Lucas followed the airplane's noisy path, toward the hangar and flight
crew quarters.

''They're staying,'' he told her.

She sagged against him in momentary defeat before once
again straightening away. ''Nothing's ever been easy,'' she
said. ''Why did I think this might be?''

''Come with me,'' he said.

''But—''

''We have only minutes before they come through the terminal,'' he said. ''Now, Meg. Come with me.''

She glanced at the car. ''I'll see that it's returned,'' he told
her. ''You don't need to drive tonight. Come with me,
Meg.''

She looked at him steadily, and he knew she saw more than he meant for her to see: the invitation he was helpless to resist giving her for more, much more than a ride home.

Now she lifted her hand to his cheek and held him immobile until other sounds from the runway intruded on their solitude. She smiled, reluctantly and wistfully, and dropped her hand. "Yes," she said. "I will."

Lucas's house was an unlighted white monolith, gilded by the moon on its graceful, landscaped knoll. He pulled to a stop in the front drive, and Megan looked up at dark windows.

"Will we wake Jamie?" she asked.

"No." Lucas turned off the engine and removed the key. "I didn't know how late I'd be, so I sent her to Marianna's tonight."

Meg swallowed once. No chaperone, even an unwitting one, waited in the house. Well, wasn't that what she wanted? Hadn't she wanted it from almost the day she'd met Lucas Lambert? "I...I see. She told me today that Marianna is her aunt?"

"It's a little more complicated than that. Marianna and Jamie's mother were cousins."

"I...I see."

"Damn it!" The words erupted from him, and he jabbed the key into the ignition.

"What are you doing?"

"What I should have done to start with. I'm taking you home."

"No." She reached across the console and removed the key, and then, not waiting for him, she opened her door and stepped out into the night.

She heard his car door slam and she heard her heart thudding against her ribs as she walked across the lawn and stepped onto the wide flat porch that graced his house. That was all she heard over the roaring of her own fear and indecision. Was she doing the right thing? He wanted her—he *had* wanted her—she couldn't doubt that. But for how long, she had no idea. Never mind. He wanted her. For the first time in her life someone really wanted her. And for the first time in her life she had the strength to act on what she wanted.

He opened the door for her and immediately punched out numbers on a security panel much like the one she'd seen by his back door. He took her cape from her, hung it on a stylized coat tree and ushered her into a spacious, almost Spartanly furnished living room. He lit a match to the firewood and kindling waiting in a wide, white fireplace and gestured toward a comfortable-looking, overstuffed but streamlined sofa. "I have to make some calls," he told her. "To...to check in."

She nodded, and he left the room.

Meg caught her hands to her mouth. God! What was she doing?

She was doing what she wanted, perhaps for the first time. She was doing what both of them wanted. And she had every right to do it.

Didn't she?

Gradually she became aware of the room. Spartanly furnished it might be, but everything in it was in exquisite taste, straight out of a 1930s *Architectural Digest,* if the magazine had in fact existed at that time. Small treasures graced the stark, clean lines of the tables and built-in bookcases, and what treasures they were—small graceful bronzes, an exquisitely shaped natural crystal, an intricately carved fan with each individual blade a subtly varied shade of jade. Lucas's life might not be cluttered, but it was far from bare.

Or barren.

What had ever made her think it was?

Had he lived here with Jamie's mother? Had she selected these exquisite treasures, thinking that she would be here to share them with him for—forever? Had she been small and delicate like these treasures? Like...like Jennie?

She whirled around to face the now crackling fire. She wouldn't think about them, about tiny, feminine, confident women. And she wouldn't do anything else to make Lucas think of them. Tonight—at least tonight—was her night, her night to know what it meant for a loving, caring man to want her. To need her.

He returned carrying two stemmed glasses. "There's enough of a chill tonight, I thought you might enjoy a brandy."

Even realizing he couldn't possibly know just what she had been thinking, Meg felt a slow flush rising. With a slight smile, she took the snifter from him. Thanks to Marianna's coaching, she recognized the heady aroma of this fine French cognac; she knew to swirl the liquid gently in the glass, to breathe in the aroma, to bring just a taste of it into her mouth and hold it there, savoring its richness before swallowing.

But Marianna's coaching hadn't covered what happened next. Would Marianna, single and really more alone now than Meg was, understand why Meg was here, why she so desperately wished for at least a facade of sophistication to help her through the next few hours? *I would die for Lucas Lambert, maybe even kill for him.* Yes, feeling like that, Marianna would definitely understand Meg's needs. But feeling like that, would she forgive them?

Lucas took her snifter from her and set it with his on the mantel. "Come with me. There's something I want to show you."

She had glimpsed a corner of the dining room through the double doorway leading into the living room, but nothing prepared her for its stark beauty. The exterior wall held banks of casement windows, partially covered now with tailored, jade green draperies and a huge octagonal inset of glass brick that would act much as an insulated skylight to bring the glory of the sun but not its heat into this spectacular room.

"Oh." Meg paused just inside the doorway, unable to go farther, unable to say more.

"Not the room, Meg." Lucas took her arm and led her into the room, pausing at the end of the table. "The mirror."

He turned her slightly, and she saw then what he meant. The two of them stood there, reflected in the purity of a seamless mirrored wall against the magnificent backdrop of his dining room: he, in another of the elegantly tailored gray suits that he wore with such flair, dark, almost menacing in appearance; she, all in black, the heels of her boots bringing her height to within an inch or two of his. A pair. Dark. Tall. Dramatic. A pair? "Oh."

He'd stepped to her side and placed his arm around her, holding her immobile with nothing but the touch of his hand on her shoulder. But he didn't have to hold her still; she stood mesmerized by his closeness and by the picture they made.

"I bought this house six years ago," he told her. "After Alicia died. I'd had enough of ruffles and clutter to last me more than a lifetime. Except for areas where Jamie is free to indulge in all the clutter and, if she should ever want, ruffles, she needs, there are none in my home. It's all clean, streamlined and beautiful. Like you, Meg. Like you."

She felt dangerously close to tears again, and a huge fist was squeezing her chest and her throat. "But I'm not," she said, needing him to know the truth. "This is all subterfuge, an image Marianna helped create."

"Did she? Or did she just help free what and who you've been all along and no one bothered to look deeply enough to see?"

She turned then, and raised her hand to his cheek, blessing him silently for the precious gift he had just given her.

His eyes darkened, and he raised his hand to her face but then burrowed it through her hair, holding her. "I can't love you," he said. His hands tightened on her, holding her captive when she would have recoiled with the pain. "No. It isn't you. It's me. A fault in me. But I need you. More than I've ever thought I would need again. And maybe, by being at least this honest about the selfish bastard I am, I won't burn too long in hell from adding my name to the long list of people who have taken from you instead of giving you the love you need and are entitled to."

Taking from her? Couldn't he see that he'd been giving since the moment they met?

Apparently not. And apparently he couldn't see that she

wouldn't—would never—reject him. He eased his fingers from her hair and dropped his hand to his side. "I...see," he said.

"No. No, you don't." She caught his hand in hers and held him when he would have turned away from her. If anyone was taking, it was Meg, greedily, hungrily, like a starving person, and she felt a moment's guilt. "Lucas," she said softly, not sure how he would receive her words, only that she must say them. "Would you—" She felt the tears forming in her eyes as her plea formed in her heart. She willed them not to fall even as she willed herself to voice her plea. "Would you show me what it's like to...to feel loved?"

He studied her silently, and then his eyes closed for a second, maybe on a prayer of his own. He took a breath that swelled his massive chest, then released it and the tension she had felt grip him with her first touch. "I can do that, Meg," he said softly as he bent his head and took the half step that was necessary to bring his lips to hers. "Oh, yes. I can do that."

Meg was sleek and supple, strong and enchantingly shy. They'd kissed their way, silent and needy, upstairs to the hermit's lair that his bedroom had become. Now she was in his bed, and Lucas was afraid she was in his heart. No one had to tell him that a careless word or act could wound Meg's fragile ego, perhaps past recovery. And no one had to tell him that even though she had been married and had borne a child, no one had ever taken the time or the care to truly make love with Meg. He spared a silent curse for Blake Wilson, and then he spared another for himself. It wasn't the same, he vowed. Even though he couldn't let himself love her, he could treasure this precious gift of her body and her trust.

If the gift didn't kill him first.

He felt her untutored hands fumbling at his throat and realized he still wore his tie and jacket. He pulled away from her long enough to jerk the tie from his neck, to shrug out of the jacket and toss them both aside. He fumbled for the switch on the bedside lamp and threw a pool of soft light across the bed.

Meg closed her eyes against the light. "No," she mumbled, reaching for the lamp.

"Yes." He caught her hand and kissed each of her fingers. "I want to see you. I want you to see me."

She opened her eyes and looked at him, and the trust and love he saw there almost did him in. "Yes," she said, and her lips, pouty and slightly swollen from his assault on them, softened in invitation. "Definitely yes."

He took her hands in his and raised them to rest on the pillow beside her head, then twisted slightly from where he sat beside her to feast at the sight of her stretched out on his tailored bedspread. "You're so beautiful. So very beautiful."

Meg gave a throaty little laugh and reached for him. Once again he caught her hands. "Not yet," he said. "The reality of you is going to be more than I ever dreamed of, but let me have my fantasy for just a moment more."

Her boots came first. With hands that trembled slightly, he reached beneath the wool crepe of her slacks to find the top of her left boot. With an indrawn breath, he eased the zipper down and tossed the boot in the general vicinity of his wool jacket. Freed, her foot rested trustingly in his hand. He traced her high arch before circling her narrow ankle with his fingers. He hissed in another breath. Silk. Her boot sock was light silk that delineated each slender bone and gentle curve. What other surprises waited for him beneath the circumspect black wool she wore?

He freed her other foot and traced his hand along the calf of her leg beneath the caressing wool, all the time watching her huge, dark eyes, which darkened even more. She moaned, and he felt his heart clench.

"Maybe I'll just grab you," she choked out. "Pull you down here and have my wicked way with you. Ravish you, if necessary."

He continued tracing a teasing pattern on the calf of her leg as he smiled at her wanton threats.

"Lucas, you're killing me. Did you know that? You're

going to drive me crazy first and then leave me in a frustrated puddle of want. Come here. Oh, please come here.''

Wisecracks, smart comments and jokes while making love. Did Meg realize how far she had come in only minutes or how free she must feel with him to risk his misunderstanding her fledgling attempts at intimate pillow talk? Maybe not. But he did. "Anything you want," he told her as he slid his hand down her leg and lowered himself to stretch along the length of her, cushioning his chest on the inviting pillow of her breasts, his almost painfully throbbing erection unmistakable against the soft valley of her thighs.

"Anything?" she rasped out.

"Anything."

"Well. It would be nice if…" She wiggled slightly, the little minx, and grinned at him to let him know she was fully aware of what she had just done to him. "It would be nice if…"

"If what, Megan?" he growled.

"If you took your boots off."

She knew that wasn't what he was expecting; her eyes danced with slumberous humor.

"Oh, hell, I'm sorry." He groaned and pushed himself off her, twisting to sit on the side of the bed and tug at boots that had suddenly become two sizes too small and didn't want to come off. They didn't want to leave the comfort of Meg's body any more than he did. He heard a slight rustling as she rose behind him, but finally the first boot came free, and he sent it sailing across the room and tugged at the second.

"And…" He heard Meg's voice, hesitant and once again shy as the second boot came free.

"And?" he asked, turning to face her.

Silk. That was what waited. Flesh colored silk. A camisole and thigh high briefs. Not sheer, hiding all but the shape of her as it draped lovingly over small, proud breasts, a waist his hands could easily span and the gentle flare of her hips. And legs. Miles of slender, shapely legs.

His breath caught in his throat and lodged there. That was

all right. He didn't need to breathe anymore; his heart had quit on him at the same time his lungs had stopped working.

"And..." She was having a little trouble with her breath, too, he noticed. "And you might as well get rid of some of those other extraneous clothes."

He dropped his boot and twisted to pull her against him. The soft silk bunched under his hands as his mouth found hers.

Starving. He had been starving all his life, and he'd almost denied himself the life-giving force this woman now shared so unselfishly with him. No. No, he'd never had a prayer of denying himself anything Meg chose to give him. No matter how hard he'd fought.

Make it good for her. Some segment of his mind continued to function as together they worked him out of his clothes and her out of the few scraps of silk. Some fragment of sanity prevailed as he lost himself in her touch and in the touch of her. Do that much for her; give her what she asked you for. Show her how it feels to be loved, he remembered, he promised, as he at last joined their aching, feverish bodies, because that, oh, yes, that was what she was doing, with every tantalizing, tormenting touch of her hands and lips. Oh, yes, that was what she was doing for him.

Heaven.

Meg felt the slide of fine cotton beneath her, the luxury of the down pillow cushioning her head, the gentle abrasion of Lucas's hands as he led her from mindlessness toward ecstasy, but most of all, she felt the welcome invasion of his body. She'd never known...never known. For a moment the knowledge of still another betrayal threatened to shatter the euphoria that Lucas was so carefully, so *lovingly* giving her. She pushed that errant and unwelcome feeling away. Later she might, probably would, explore. But not now. Now was for feeling, experiencing, sharing this shattering act of beauty.

She felt his heated breath and then his lips on her throat and arched upward yet again, meeting him as she knew he wanted but didn't demand. Lucas never demanded. Yet by not doing so, by only giving, he ensured that she would give all that was in her to meet the needs she knew he would never verbalize.

And then her thoughts quit, and only sensations surrounded them as Meg shattered beneath the onslaught of feeling, and Lucas, who couldn't love, wouldn't love, tumbled with her into a haven that only love could have created.

Ten

Lucas held her long after her tremors had ceased, caressing her, showing her a world of caring she had never allowed herself to believe existed. How strange at thirty—correction, not quite twenty-nine—however the blazes old she was!—to learn that she should have believed.

Or maybe not. Maybe believing would have made its absence unbearable.

A kernel of anger worked its way through Meg's enchanted lethargy. Even this! How much more had been denied her because of someone's greed?

Lucas murmured softly and pulled her closer, easing her head down onto his shoulder and lifting her hand to his smooth chest to rest it over the steadying beat of his heart. Soothing her. Cherishing her.

Not love her? Heaven help the woman Lucas Lambert did finally allow himself to love. She'd be destroyed within days from the sheer overload of sensation and caring—treasuring—from this man Meg had once thought she ought to be terrified of. But she hadn't been—not then, when she had barely met him, and not now, even after he had hinted at dark secrets hiding behind his civilized facade.

She felt the brush of his breath against her temple and felt the now slow, steady beat of his heart beneath her palm. He slept in her arms, her gladiator, her warrior, her lover, giving her another treasured memory. And maybe, just maybe, she had given him something, too. She knew he wouldn't want her to voice the love she felt for him—that would be a burden he couldn't easily bear—but maybe, just maybe, without the words, she had been able to show him what she had asked him to do for her—to show him how it felt to be loved.

When she awoke, he still held her wrapped tightly to the warmth of his body. Now, though, she felt prickles of unease, and when she tilted her head, she found him silently watching her.

She lifted her hand and traced his now unsmiling lips that only a short time ago had helped give her more pleasure than she had ever known. She felt her own lips lift in a welcoming smile, and knew she had to say at least this much. "Thank you."

His eyes turned bleak, and his body tensed beneath her touch. "Don't, Meg."

Don't? Don't what? Don't touch him? Don't expect him to touch her again. Wait! her clamoring emotions screamed. Lucas had never been cruel to her; he wouldn't begin now. Gathering her courage, she held onto her smile. "Don't what, Lucas?"

"Don't ever again settle for less than you're entitled to. Don't thank me for taking advantage of you."

"Excuse me?"

"You're warm and giving and loving and generous. You need someone to share those qualities with you, not feed on them."

Meg felt her hand try to clench against his chest and forced it to open. It would have been nice to ease back into the world after the magical trip she had just taken, but apparently he wasn't going to let her. But she wouldn't let him ruin the memory of that trip. "I was under the impression," she said carefully, "that there was a whole lot of sharing going on."

"I didn't protect you."

She blinked once, trying to grasp what he had just said. He'd been protecting her since the moment they met. And then his meaning became clear. Oh. She hadn't even thought of protection. But then, even if she had, would she have insisted upon it?

"I'm a big girl, Lucas," she told him, trying to keep her voice light, trying to avoid the confrontation he seemed determined to force. "I've been in the world long enough to know the dangers of unprotected sex and to take care of myself. But all right, I'll go through the drill with you. Are you promiscuous or diseased?"

"Of course not," he said on a frustrated growl.

"I didn't think so. Not for a moment. Neither am I."

"Damn it, Meg, I know you're not, but did you give any thought to the fact that right now you might be pregnant?"

Pregnant? Oh. "No."

"I should be whipped for putting you at risk."

"Wait just a minute." Meg caught his shoulder as he tried to roll away from her. "Let me repeat this. I am an adult, Lucas Lambert, and as such, I am responsible for my own actions."

"Right. And so experienced. Tell me, Meg. Have you ever made love outside of your marriage bed?"

She could only stare at him, not speaking. After what he had shown her tonight, she knew that she had never made love before, not even in her marriage bed.

"I thought not. And what would an unwanted child do to your new life, Meg?"

Unwanted? How could he think that any child she bore, especially his child, would be unwanted? "Enrich it," she told him. "Enchant it."

He groaned again, and this time he succeeded in rolling away from her. He sat up and swung his legs over the side of the bed, sitting tense and unyielding with his back to her. Meg lifted her hand to his shoulder and felt him flinch.

Be careful, she warned herself, because she realized there were forces at work here that had nothing to do with the wonderful cherishing moments they had just shared, nothing to do with her, but that could shatter both.

"I was under the impression that we shared something beautiful, and as necessary to me as food or air. What happened while I slept to change all that, Lucas?"

"You just don't get it, do you?"

"No." She heard her voice rising and forced it to a semblance of calm. "No, I don't. Why don't you explain it to me?"

"You don't need to settle for any less than the best, Meg. You don't have to ask for love anymore. You should never have had to ask. You're Meg Carlton, now. Rich as well as beautiful and intelligent. You have a whole new life spread out in front of you, a whole new series of possibilities just waiting for you. You don't need to tie yourself to me through any misguided sense of loyalty or gratitude or—"

"Wait just a minute." Now her hand did clench, and now her voice did rise. "I'd never tie you to me. I thought you had enough sense to realize that. And as for misguided— why don't you let me figure out just exactly what it is I'm feeling before you try to tell me? All right? And while we're dissecting my emotions, why don't you tell me what happened in the last few minutes to make you so intent on beating up on yourself?"

He turned then, and took her hand in his. Gently he opened her fingers and caressed her palm. Then he traced a tear she hadn't been aware of in its path down her cheek.

"All right," he said at last. "I owe you that much."

"You don't owe me—"

"Hush," he said. "Don't look at me like that." He pulled her close and hid her face against his shoulder. "Let me hold you."

"Lucas, you don't have to—"

"Yes." She felt his hand at the back of her head gentle in a caress, felt his other hand trace a soothing pattern across her back. Even drawn tight as a catapult about to release its load of rock and shrapnel, he gave her comfort. "Yes, I do."

He drew in a deep breath and released it, but remained silent for so long she knew he must be sorting through too many memories for one person to have to bear.

"My father is Harrison Lambert," he said at last. "Yes," he said when she tensed. "I see you've heard of him. Cable TV and construction companies, corporate takeovers and championship racehorses, and a new movie star on his arm each year—I hear he's trying to buy a major television network again and may just make it this time—and a lineage he can trace back to the founding families of the Commonwealth of Virginia." He chuckled, but she heard no humor in his flat recitation of facts. "As well as a couple of other lineages that go back to the Irish potato famine and the conquered American West, but he doesn't like to acknowledge those.

"Just as he didn't like to acknowledge a wife who had severe depression and a growing drinking problem, or a son who refused to follow in his footsteps. That was all right, though. He had several houses in the country where he could hide his wife when she wasn't a fit companion for his old-money aristocracy and new-money CEO image, and he had another son coming along that he could shape into his own image.

"I met Alicia during my senior year at the University of Virginia where I studied criminology—another of my rebellions. My father had wanted me at Harvard, or he would have settled for Yale. Law or political science or even medicine would have been acceptable, but an MBA was his real goal for me so that when I came to my senses I could step into my rightful place as his second in command. But by then my mother's parents, who had never liked my father, had established trust funds—small ones—for both me and my younger brother, Lyle, so I was pretty much able to tell the old man to take a flying leap.

"My roommate was a childhood friend, Trent Dawson." Again he chuckled, this time a little more warmly, and traced another circle across her back. His words came easier now, or perhaps just faster. She forced herself to remain silent. "Yes, the FBI agent you met. Trent was there in ROTC and prelaw on a scholarship and was already committed to a military career, at least for enough years to repay his education.

"Four of us went to Padre Island on our spring break— our Virginia beaches suddenly weren't exotic enough for us. Alicia was there from Vassar with three of her sorority sisters.

"She was so different from the kind of women I'd known all my life. Even though it was obvious she came from money, she had the kind of forthrightness I'd always associated with Westerners, frontierspeople, or I thought she did, but she was also small and delicate, as fragile as the Southern women in my circles, who are raised knowing how to give that appearance.

"We continued to see each other after we returned to classes, flying and driving back and forth on weekends. She told me she loved me. I began to believe she might.

"I had always thought the ultimate irony in light of my father's plans would be for me to take a police commission in some small town and work my way up through the ranks from patrolman to—well to whatever. But by then I'd been talking with an FBI recruiter. At that time they required agents to have either a degree in law or accounting. I knew I didn't want to go on to law school, so I had decided to go for a master's in accounting. I'd just finished my first semester in grad school when I realized it didn't meet with Alicia's plans, which, slow learner that I am, I finally discovered included a wedding ring, a big plantation-style house and a nanny or two to raise the new heir she and I would produce after a suitable time of enjoying my rightful position as my father's successor. I saw this as the ultimate betrayal. She insisted she only wanted me to have what was due me.

"I don't know. Maybe the wedding ring and kids would have been enough for her. Maybe a commitment from me would have been enough. But I couldn't give her one, and now I'll never know. Can you understand that, Meg? She was the one person in my life who swore she loved me. Perhaps if I had given her the time then, she might have one day actually done so. But no, I couldn't do that.''

Did he know how much disappointment his voice showed he still carried? Maybe not. But it was disappointment in himself she heard, and not in the betrayal he had should have felt from someone who obviously shared a great portion of the responsibility for that disappointment. Meg wanted to stop him, but she knew she shouldn't. Instead she slid her arms around him and held him more tightly. She felt him sigh against her.

"About that time, my father decided my mother had become too big a liability for the political image he was building. He also decided on a big party to announce he was surrendering a large block of stock to my brother—to reward him for being a dutiful son. Although that wasn't announced publicly, it was to the family. I'd failed him by my choice of career and by choosing to spend what limited time I spent with my family with my mother—his biggest failure. I'd argued with Lyle and finally accused him of selling out to the old man. I was invited to the party, but I couldn't be bothered to go. My mother wasn't invited. She was supposed to be stashed safely away in the care of the last of a long succession of nurses who over the years had grown more and more to resemble jailers. I arrived to visit with her only to learn that she'd escaped from her keeper. By the time I put all the pieces together, it was too late.

"The rest is speculation and gossip, but apparently Lyle saw her as she arrived at his party. They had words—some say he swore she wouldn't ruin his evening. Others say he was genuinely concerned for her. I hope to God it was the latter. I hope he hadn't really become the man I had accused him of becoming. In any event, he left with her, to take her home. They never made it. Somehow on a clear bright night, with no traffic, he wrapped his car around a telephone pole. Both of them were dead before they reached the hospital.

"My father called me. He said, 'Your mother killed my son.'''

"Oh, no. No, he didn't," Meg said on a moan. "He couldn't have." She felt the tremor work its way through him and understood what he wasn't saying. "No, Lucas," she said. "It wasn't your fault. None of it was your fault." She tried to pull away from him—just far enough so that she could touch his face, that she could comfort him, but he wouldn't let her go.

"There's more," he said. "God help me, there's more."

Meg worked her hand between them to rest it over his heart and forced herself to be still. She'd asked for this. No, she had demanded this, and she knew there was no way he could stop the torment she had unleashed.

"Trent had graduated and been sworn into the Army. He'd trained that summer and started law school in the fall—the military still did that for those they really wanted. A week after my mother's funeral, two men stopped me outside my apartment. Trent had given them my name. They'd reviewed my FBI application and school record and made a decision based on my appearance—I could be a chameleon in any number of hot spots in the world—my aptitude for languages, my size and strength, and most of all, I believe now, my absolute conviction that I had nothing in the world to lose."

"Oh, Lucas. No."

"I told myself this was a way I could repay in part the selfishness of my life up to that point, and for a while I believed it. For a while I was damned good at ferreting out known terrorists and luring them into situations where they could be captured, in thwarting plans, in locating hostages, in soothing over potential problems. So good that after a while I began believing my own hype, I began believing that I was invincible, invaluable, indestructible. See the pattern?"

She shook her head against his chest, wanting to weep for him, but knowing she couldn't let him feel her tears.

"I was in the Middle East—it doesn't matter where now, because the village no longer exists. I'd been spotted trying to get out of the area after I'd made contact with an informant to gather information about black market nuclear weapons.

I'd been wounded. A woman in the village, an amazing, courageous young woman, whom I knew only as Star, hid me in a nearby cave and went in my place to find my emergency contact. The entire village took turns seeing to my needs, bringing me food, changing my bandages or just sitting with me while the fever raged through me. One, a boy about Danny's age, wanted to know about baseball. Every time he came, he laughed with me about one day playing on a real team.

"I heard the trucks pull into the village one day. I managed to drag myself to the door of the cave just as the search began, just as they herded every villager into the tiny square. They brought Star with them, more dead than alive. I heard the machine guns, and then I saw the fires, and I knew it was only a matter of moments before they came for me.

"No one ever came.

"There were twenty-seven people in that village, Meg—women, children and old men. All twenty-seven died that day keeping the secret of the whereabouts of my worthless hide."

"And the information you had acquired? Didn't they protect that, too?"

He swore, briefly, succinctly. "Any of them could have carried it out."

She held him. He was not aware of it, but she rocked with him, holding him, letting him spew it out.

"Star had been captured returning to the village. My contact had not been. Eventually he arrived and hauled me to safety. Back in the States, while I was recovering, Trent visited me. We'd worked together more than once since I'd been recruited. It seemed those two recruiters had been after him, too. They just waited longer to sign him on. While I was hiding in a cave, Trent had been on leave, and he'd caught up with some old friends.

"Alicia was bitter when she left me, more bitter than I had any reason to suspect, more angry than any human should be and more secretive than I thought it possible for her to be. But she'd slipped, in a conversation with one of her sorority sisters, or maybe she hadn't slipped. Maybe she'd wanted the news to get back to me, but she hadn't known it would take more than seven years for Trent to talk to that one woman and then to come to me with a reason to go on living.

"I found my daughter in Avalon, living with Marianna and her father, and Alicia. Alicia was even more bitter than when she'd left, this time with more reason. She was ill, very ill. They'd found a nasty little tumor in her brain, and in trying to get it out had messed up a couple of major functions in addition to not retrieving all of the cancer. Eight years too late I gave her the ring she wanted. Eight years too late, I acknowledged the child she gave me. She lived for one more year."

Meg closed her eyes against his chest and released her breath in one long, quivering sigh. No wonder Lucas looked battered; no wonder he looked as though he had never been cherished. Before Jamie, had there ever been any softness in his life? Before tonight, had he ever had anyone to share the hell he'd endured? And how, having been raised in a loveless home and having spent all his formative years in the sewers of the world had he become the sensitive, caring man that she loved? And knowing what he had been through, how could she keep herself from telling him how she felt?

She eased her arms from around him and leaned back until she could raise her hands to cup his face, until she could see his eyes.

Bleak. More bleak even than they had been when she awoke to found him watching her, his eyes told her he waited for her rejection. "I love you," she said.

She saw the blow of her words strike him. Then slowly he took her hands, dragged them from his cheeks and held them tightly before releasing them. "I've never been of value to anyone in my entire life," he said. "Never once, when someone who loved me needed me, have I been there."

Could he believe that? "It seems to me that you tried to be, with both your brother and your mother. It certainly seems to me that you stood by Alicia. I know that Jamie thinks you hung the moon. And if no one can count on you, why did Marianna tell me she'd be willing to die for you?"

"Marianna is intensely loyal to family and friends. That's one of the reasons we love her."

Family. Friends. Not lovers. But hadn't Meg already known that on some level? Just as she now knew Lucas would not divulge what he had done to earn that loyalty.

"You have love in your life, Lucas. It's time for you to let yourself see it. It's time for you to let yourself feel it. You owe it to yourself to—"

"I have no life, Meg."

He stood and turned away from her. "Not one that is mine. I owe that life to the memory of twenty-seven people who seemed to think I was worth saving. And that's a debt too great ever to repay. I make interest payments only, helping where I can, doing what I can. But I'll never be free of that debt. And I'll never be free to consider what, if anything, I owe myself."

Suddenly aware that she knelt naked on the edge of a bed, pleading with a man to accept her love, Meg drew the sheet around her. "Is that what I was?" she asked. "An interest payment?"

"No. God, no." Lucas shuddered and reached for a maroon-colored robe that lay tangled in the covers at the foot of the bed. "No. It's getting late. We'd better get dressed. We don't want to have to explain to Danny why we were out all night."

Lucas pulled to a stop at the locked security gates in front of Edward's house. "What are your plans for today?"

Oh, yes, he was very much once again the sheriff. Meg felt an almost hysterical laugh bubble up. She fought it down. She didn't know if she would be nearly so successful fighting back the sob she felt building. "Not many," she said. "Danny wanted to go back out to visit Mrs. Tompkins's nephew at the ranch, but I suppose we could put that off."

"No. That's fine. It might be a good idea for you to go with him, for both of you to get out of the house. I'll have to keep in touch with the office, but otherwise I'm free. I'll take you."

Take you. Watch over you. Protect you. I just can't love you. Meg heard all that in what he said and what he didn't say.

"That isn't necessary."

"Yes," he said. "It is."

Mrs. Tompkins met them at the front door. "Danny's awake, Ms. Wilson," she said, "but I don't believe he knows yet that you aren't at home." She turned toward Lucas. "And Paul Slater wants you to call him as soon as possible."

While Meg went to speak to Danny, Lucas used the telephone in Edward's study to return Slater's call.

"Daddy Wilson got a phone call a little while ago," Slater said when Lucas reached him at his office.

"I don't think I want to know how you know that."

"Nope. I didn't think so, either. But you do want to know that he booked a flight into Albuquerque and reserved a car to be waiting for him there. It seems that some people just don't take kindly to being chauffeured around in luxury vans and made to stay in a hundred-year-old, five-star lodge. It seems those folks at least want wheels of their own."

"Sounds reasonable to me," Lucas said, but then his voice hardened and he abandoned any attempt at humor. "I was hoping for a little more time before they got mobile. It's an odd crew, Paul. Wilson and the Stemples never got along, and now they're teamed up thicker than thieves. Maybe it does make sense in an odd sort of way. Maybe in addition to transportation, Blake wanted a player on his side."

"Maybe," Paul admitted, "but here's something else to throw in that cauldron you've got bubbling out there, something else you didn't hear from me. Blake didn't call his daddy. Audrey did."

"Damn!" Lucas sank back in his chair. "Paul?"

"Yeah. I know. Everything we've already learned says there's no way in hell those two should be talking."

"What do we have on him?"

"Not much. Until now, he's been way down on the play list."

"Get it."

"Right. How far back to you want to go?"

"As far as it takes to find some connection. And, Paul?"

"Yeah."

"Contact Trent Dawson. He's not going to be able to share a lot, but this might trigger something in their investigation."

Meg debated changing clothes before she sought out Danny but abandoned that idea. She was through with playing games and avoiding problems.

He looked up from his cereal and frowned when she came into the room. "Wow, this is a first."

Meg rounded the table and pulled out a chair beside him. Mrs. Tompkins placed a cup of coffee in front of her and made a strategic retreat from the room. "What is?"

"This is the first time you've had to wear the same thing twice since we got here. Does this mean we're broke again?"

So much for the rapport she'd thought they'd regained the afternoon before. "I've been out already this morning, Danny."

"Yeah. I know. With *him*."

She didn't pretend to misunderstand. "Yes. We had something very important to discuss."

And she had something important to discuss with her son, but first there was something else she had to do, something she'd put off much too long because in addition to hoping his naturally sunny disposition would help him work his way through his resentment, she truly hadn't known how to reach him. Her talks with Mrs. Tompkins the day before had finally given her an idea of how to begin. Mrs. Tompkins had seen the parallels; so had Meg. Now it was time for her to help Danny see them.

She sat down and picked up her cup. "Tell me about Skeeter."

"Skeeter? You've been out playing kiss-face with the local law and you want me to tell you about a stray dog?"

Meg winced at Danny's too perceptive, crude comment, but she refused to be baited away from a subject that had to be explored.

"Yes. I do. But not just any dog. I want you to tell me everything you know about one particular stray yellow hound."

It was like pulling teeth. Danny glared at his cereal, holding on to his resentment. "You could start by telling me about her name," she suggested. "It isn't your everyday Rover, Spot or Lassie. Mrs. Tompkins said she thought it was short for Mosquito. I wonder why anyone would name a dog after a nasty little bug."

"'Cause she's fast," Danny mumbled.

"Fast?"

Danny surrendered his spoon and turned to face her. "Yeah. Fast. Like a mosquito when you go to swat it, you know, only it's gone by the time you swing."

Meg studied her cup. "And does she have reason to be fast?"

"Yeah. Look, I know what you're doing. So somebody kicked her, all right. Maybe more than once. Maybe a lot. But I'm not a dumb old dog hiding out in a barn. I know who did the kicking. I'm not afraid of everyone like she is. I know who my friends are, and right now, I figure that's you. Period. Maybe. Unless you've decided you like that sheriff a lot more than you do me."

She couldn't let him see how his words hurt her; she knew they came from pain. But it was time for him to let go of that pain, to reach out before he curled completely in on himself.

"And Jamie?" she asked. "Isn't she a friend?"

"Well, yeah. Maybe."

"And Edward and Jennie? They didn't have to leave us here in their house. Edward doesn't have to check with us every day even though, as we both know, he's got to be worried sick about Jennie. Edward's been hurt, too. It seems to me he's a lot more like your new friend than like the one who mistreated her."

"And *your* new friend, Mom. The sheriff? I suppose you're going to tell me he never kicked a dog in his life?"

If there was one undeniable fact about her son, it was that he was an extremely bright kid. He might not always like the conclusions he drew, but he was sure able to draw them. "That's right, Danny. That's exactly what I'm telling you. You'd have seen it yourself if you hadn't been so busy snapping and snarling at people who just want to love you and be your friend."

"That's what he said," Danny muttered.

"Who?"

"Your buddy, the sheriff." Danny sighed and slumped in his chair. "The other day when I had the fight with Jamie."

Lucas had spoken with Danny the day he ran out of the house? That was news to her. But was it so surprising? "And how did he say it, Danny? Did he grab you, shake you, yell at you?"

"No. He just talked to me. Kind of like you do." Danny slid a look at her face. "I guess that must have been a clue, huh?"

She couldn't help herself. At twelve, Danny insisted he was too old for hugs and mushy stuff; she only got them when she told him they were for her benefit. This was for both of them. She took him in her arms and squeezed him tight and was rewarded by his answering squeeze and awkward pat.

"So what do I have to do?" Danny asked when he pulled away from her. "Apologize to everybody, or what?"

Meg shook her head. "Just give them a chance, Danny. You might find there's a lot to like about this place."

"Him, too?"

Meg nodded. "Him, too."

"All right. But you've got to know I'm not going to like it."

No, but he'd do it. For her. And he had absolutely no idea how much like this man he professed not to trust he was.

And now if she wasn't careful, she'd throw him right back into the sour and bitter mood he'd been in for so long.

"I have to tell you something," she said.

He seemed to sense bad news coming; he tensed and watched her warily.

"It's what Lucas and I were discussing. It's why I went out last night." He wasn't going to make it easy for her. "Your dad has found us."

"Oh, gee, Ma." His voice broke. "Does he have to spoil this, too?"

"No." This she could promise him. "This time he's not going to spoil anything. But he and the people who adopted me chartered a plane, and last night they arrived. They're at the Lodge now, waiting for me to decide if I will see them."

"You can do that? Just not see them. And they'll go away?"

"Maybe," she admitted.

"What about Jamie's dad? He's the law here. If you tell him to, will he make them leave?"

From villain to hero in the space of seconds. She wondered if Lucas would appreciate the black humor in Danny's about-face.

"Maybe," she said. "Maybe. But for today he's going to do something just as important. Today he's taking us out to this ranch you're so fond of and making sure that they—the Stemples and your dad—don't try to push the issue and see us before I make up my mind."

Eleven

Lucas didn't want to interrupt Meg's talk with Danny. He didn't want to give her son any more ammunition to use in his fight to be dissatisfied with his mom's new life, and he sensed that confronting him at this hour of the morning could do just that. Instead, he sought out Tommy. "Tell Meg I'll be back in an hour or so," he said when he'd finished filling her in on the latest developments so that she could alert the household security staff. "That will give her time to freshen up and have breakfast and finish this round with her son."

Tommy gave him a wise and knowing grin that only someone of long acquaintance would dare with him. "Sometimes it feels as though there ought to be a referee and a bell permanently attached to that boy, doesn't it?"

"Watch it, woman," he said without heat, "or you'll be looking for another two-cop town to police."

Tommy chuckled. "And leave you with the sole responsibility of the security firm? I don't think so." Her humor faded. "You're on to something, aren't you?"

"I don't know," Lucas admitted. "But suddenly there are

way too many pieces in this pie. I need to do some checking at the office. I won't be long. But with Wilson coming in by car, I'm not sure it will be wise to take Meg and Danny out to the ranch.''

''My sister's family won't be home until after church, so there's no need to make a decision right this moment. Maybe by noon, some of those pieces will have settled into place.''

But an hour later they hadn't.

Lucas had built a file on Edward Carlton when Edward had arrived in Avalon claiming that Jennie was his wife. Edward had contributed to it when it began to appear that Jennie had not left him but had instead been a victim of the kind of greed that had deprived Edward of his parents and sister. Although what had happened to Jennie was not relevant now, most of the file was.

Lucas opened a map of California and spread it out on his desk. A circle marked the location of the friend's home where Meg's parents had planned to vacation but where only signs of a minor struggle, and a telling splattering of blood, had marked their arrival; another, slightly to the south, where their bodies had been found. He added a third circle around the town of Simonville, far from the coast, in the foothills of the mountains north and east of Sacramento, but almost on a direct line from the second circle.

How had a three-year-old gotten from the second circle to the third?

How had a child who had been torn from obviously loving parents wound up in the custodial care of two cold and grasping, calculating characters like James and Audrey?

Edward's statement in this file was from the perspective of a man looking back twenty-five years to the turmoil of a child. Lucas lifted it from the folder and scanned through it. *I was supposed to have gone, but at the last minute...*

The elder Carltons had left something else besides Edward behind that day. They had not taken the *Lady B*, the sailboat Edward swore that his parents loved as much as he did and which they had planned to take until they discovered a damaged mast. Had the boat been deliberately disabled?

Why? Because in it they might have been inaccessible to their attackers?

Or had whoever done this merely followed and watched and waited to make a move until the family was vulnerable?

No one had pushed that point twenty-five years ago. No one had pushed a number of points back then.

Too many pieces. And yet not enough.

Lucas glanced at his watch and grimaced. No matter what the time difference, he needed more information. He reached for his telephone and punched out the numbers on the notepad beside it.

"Carlton." Edward answered on the second ring.

"I'm sorry to bother you, but—"

"Lucas." Edward interrupted his apology. "You wouldn't if you didn't have to. Is Meggie all right?"

Was she? After last night, would she ever be? But that wasn't the question her brother was asking. "Yes. And she'll not forgive me if I don't ask you how Jennie is."

"She won't?" Edward asked. "Or is it maybe the entire town that won't?" His voice eased slightly, but his attempt at humor seemed even more strained than normal for this taciturn man. He didn't wait for an answer. "Tell her—tell her that Jennie sends her love. Tell her that she's had her surgery—"

"What!"

"She didn't want anyone to worry any more than necessary—"

"How is she?"

Edward's voice broke. "She just came back to the intensive care unit from the recovery room. The doctor told us she's doing well. Really well. It looks good."

"Thank God."

"Yes. Sometimes, Lucas, I feel as though I've spent my whole life at the whim of events over which I have no control. Because of that, I've fought for control, needing it, no trusting or believing in anything that wasn't of my doing But today, holding her hand, knowing Jennie would once again have her art and her color, and I would have her,

knew that nothing in my control had brought Jennie into my
life. I also knew I'd be a fool to deny the gift, the miracle,
that brought her back to me, because I had nothing to do
with it.

"Now, tell me." Edward made an abrupt transition back
to the businessman respected and sometimes feared through-
out the world, and Lucas honored his need to do so. "What
prompted this call? Did the cartel arrive? Does Meg want to
leave?"

Lucas proceeded to recount the events of Meg's confrontation the previous evening.

His pride in her swelled, even though he knew he had no
right to feel it.

"Did they leave?"

Lucas crashed back to the present. He had a job to do, and
losing himself in thoughts of Meg wouldn't get it done.

"No." Quickly he filled Edward in on the rest of the confrontation at the airport and on the contents of Paul Slater's
telephone call, omitting, with only a twinge of guilt, all that
had happened between those two events.

"So Blake's daddy's coming, too," Edward said reflec-
tively. "Like dogs after a bone?"

"Maybe. But with Audrey being the one to call, I'm not
sure. I know you don't want to do this, and I wouldn't ask
if I knew any way not to, but I want you to think back and
tell me everything you can remember of the events leading
up to your parents' final vacation."

"Oh, God," Edward said on a whisper. "Will it never be
over?"

"Not until we know who did it and why," Lucas said.
"Not until whoever did it is made to answer for his actions."

He wasn't there.

Meg went looking for Lucas after she left Danny. When
she didn't find him in the study, she looked outside and saw
that his car was gone. Had he been called away? Or had he
escaped? Did it matter? He'd withdrawn from her long before they left his house.

Withdrawn, not abandoned. Lucas had said he'd spend the day with her, keeping her out of harm's way. Whether it was necessary for him to do so was irrelevant; he had said he would, therefore, he would. Feeling slightly fortified by that conclusion, Meg did what she suspected she should have learned to do long ago: she went looking for Mrs. Tompkins.

Red. Meg yanked the outfit from her closet: soft, flowing red crepe slacks, a long, belted tunic of the same fabric, a silk long-sleeved turtleneck, and heels. Three-inch, high-heeled boots of soft, supple Italian leather. Red for power, for wealth, for confidence. Yes, definitely red.

Not for the first time, Meg thanked Marianna for the facade her new wardrobe and hairstyle and makeup gave her. Her adoptive parents had not liked Blake or his father. That they would band together against her was another of the knife-thrust surprises that life had proved so very competent at hurling at her. But thanks to Marianna, she would be able to look down at them— literally, figuratively and in all ways that counted. And there was no way she'd ever let them know that they still had the power to hurt her.

She smiled grimly as she tugged on her boots and settled the flowing legs of her slacks over them. From her height, she'd look down on anybody, except perhaps her brother and, of course Lucas. Lucas. He'd protect her from this confrontation if she'd let him. He'd take it on himself and someway he'd see that she never had to be subjected to any of them ever again. *He'd stand beside you, if you'd let him.* Meg hushed the noisy little voice in her head. Lucas wouldn't stand beside her; he'd stand between her and any unpleasantness or danger, and she couldn't let him do that. He'd deflected too many blows onto himself; he carried too heavy a burden to take on any of hers. And what was hers, anyway? It was inconsequential in the face of the pain he had already endured.

A glance out the window showed her the minivan had been returned. Using the telephone on her fragile desk, she dialed the number for the Lodge and asked for Norris Huxtable. His comfortably cultured voice and quick cooperation eased some of the tension building in Meg, and she gentled her words, for him, but not the message he was to relay. He was to direct his unwilling guests to be assembled and waiting for her arrival, because she would not—would never again—wait for them.

Then, because Meg had managed to learn a bit of common sense in the years she had been on her own, she sought out Mrs. Tompkins, finding her near the security staff's office, to tell her where she was going and when to expect her return.

"But Ms. Wilson, the sheriff—"

"Carlton," Meg said softly, knowing at least this much. "My name is Carlton. And this has to be my decision, not Lucas's."

Mrs. Tompkins's quick and approving smile warmed a little more of the tension in Meg. "Yes, Miss Carlton. But the sheriff just phoned. He should be here any minute. Are you sure you don't want to wait for him to go with you?"

She did want to, but Meg knew there was no way she could. She shook her head in a defiant gesture meant more to assure her than to answer any question. "No. These are my ghosts." Hanging unspoken between them were the words *Lucas has enough of his own,* and Meg had no doubt Mrs. Tompkins heard them as clearly as she did. "I should have faced them years ago."

Meg drove to the private entrance on the south side of the Lodge, but it wasn't Norris Huxtable who greeted her. Lucas stepped from the doorway and opened the door to the minivan.

"Tommy caught me by radio," he said in answer to her unspoken question. "You don't have to do this alone."

She looked at him, begging silently that he understand. "Yes. I do."

He watched her for a moment, then pulled her into a fierce hug. "All right," he told her. "We'll do it your way."

The tension returned. Even the warm grasp of his hand on

hers couldn't keep it at bay as she went with him withou
further words through a wide hallway and into a beautifull
imposing private salon—an empty salon. Meg fought to keep
her shoulders from slumping. Of course they weren't waiting
for her; never in her life had they ever done anything at her
convenience. Why should finding she had inherited half the
wealth of the free world make that any different? Because
they wanted it—all of it, or part of it, or control of it. For
the first time in her memory, she had something they cov-
eted.

Lucas took her cape and draped it over the back of one o
the two chairs facing a marble fireplace. "Norris has you
supplicants cooling their heels in the dining hall. He though
this room would be appropriate for their audience with you.'

Meg saw the concern in his eyes and reached again fo
the comfort of his hand. For him? For herself? She didn'
know, and right now she didn't seem to be able to separate
the two. She glanced over the room. "It's lovely," she said

"He thought you would like it. He asked me to tell yo
that the Late Duchess of Windsor preferred this to any of the
Lodge's other small sitting rooms."

The Duchess of Windsor. Here? In Avalon? But why not
It seemed that anything was possible in this mountain refuge
Meg glanced at the silver tea service arranged on a table
beside the chair where Lucas had placed her cape. One—
only one—perfect bone china cup and saucer waited for her
placed there by someone who knew the politics of power.

She poured tea into the solitary cup and carried it to the
fireplace. Wallis Simpson, who became the Duchess o
Windsor, had confronted the royalty of Europe; Meg had
only to face the ghosts of her past.

"I'd hoped you'd want to stand there."

He was right of course. Meg immediately visualized the
impact she would make greeting those who had always used
their strength and power against her. But suddenly Meg wa
tired of the subterfuge. She wasn't strong, and she wasn'
cruel; all she had ever wanted from the three vultures now
waiting to see her was for them to do what their places in

her life should have ensured. All she had wanted was their love.

And she would never have that.

The concern was back in Lucas's eyes. Meg summoned up a smile for him. She wouldn't have him fighting this battle. "I almost sense Marianna's fine touch in these arrangements."

She saw a small glimmer of humor before Lucas suppressed it, once again all sheriff. He lifted his hand to the mantel and pointed out a small button. "This rings into a nearby alcove. I'll have Norris summon your visitors now, but if you need help of any kind, use that bell."

Meg nodded once, abruptly.

"One at a time, or all in a pack?"

Confused, Meg looked at Lucas. Maybe not *all* sheriff. He lifted his hand and for a moment she longed to lean forward, to feel his strong hand cradling her face or pulling her into another embrace.

Meg saw his hesitation just before he dropped his hand. He was leaving her to face her demons, knowing that her physical safety was protected, but also knowing how fragile she was emotionally. He was leaving, because he must know, as she did, that she had to get beyond this confrontation before she could truly be the woman she was meant to be.

"Do you want to see them one at a time, or together?"

Heaven help the woman Lucas Lambert loved, Meg thought again. She spared a fleeting moment for jealousy of that unknown woman, knowing it wouldn't be her, and found a smile for him, for all that he had given her and all that he had done for her, and all the good in him that he couldn't see. "Together please. I don't think I can go through this more than once."

She was standing with her back to the room when she heard a quiet click as the door opened and Norris's voice as he ushered the cartel into the room. She didn't hear the click of the door closing, which meant he hadn't completely closed it. Lucas's orders? Probably. But Meg recognized the sense behind them.

She heard the other noises in the room behind her, those of people determined to force a confrontation but, probably for the first time in their lives, not sure how to begin.

Meg turned at last to look at them. There were other chairs, even what appeared to be a genuine Chippendale settee across the room, but only the intimate grouping of two close to where she stood. Meg neither sat nor invited them to. Nor did she speak. Schooled in the protocol and decorum of politics, neither James nor Audrey sat. Blake apparently had never been through the drill. He plopped himself on a fragile chair and gave her a not-quite-leering, very complete, physical appraisal, the kind he had always used to intimidate her. Then, realizing that he would have to look up to her, he popped up like a jack-in-the-box. To cover his uneasiness when she didn't cower before his inspection, he began a visual inventory of the room.

Audrey was busy inventorying Meg's wardrobe and new aura of sophistication.

James, the judge, always the judge, merely studied her with the same uncompromising disapproval he had never failed to show when she didn't measure up to his exacting standards. What had she ever done to him to deserve that kind of condemnation?

Nothing. She had done nothing. Just as her son had done nothing to deserve his father's abuse.

"Aren't you going to speak to us?"

Audrey's voice carried a hint of chastisement—not as much as when Meg had been a helpless child, but enough to tell her that in spite of the older woman's efforts to cage her temper, it still lurked about, waiting to make a bid for freedom.

Suddenly all the things she had stored up over the years, rehearsing in vulnerable moments, wanting to say to these people who had betrayed her, needing to say to them, no longer seemed necessary. Spilling out her pain to them would only give them more of a sense of victory than they deserved. Spilling out her pain to them would never ease the pain.

"I was under the impression you wanted to speak to me."

"Margaret Ann—"

This much she would do. "Meg. Margaret Ann Stemple no longer exists, if in fact she ever did. My name is Meg Carlton."

"Congratulations, Meg." Blake gave her another of his denigrating appraisals. "It's a nice scam. One of the best I've seen. How long do you think you'll be able to pull it off?"

"Shut up, Blake." James's voice carried all the authority of his years in the courtroom, surprising her, and surprising Blake enough so that he dropped that line of questioning. Could he doubt who she was? Could anyone in this room doubt her identity?

No. Blake proved that with his next tack. "I suppose you're going to use this to continue to keep my son from me."

"Oh, Blake, do be quiet," Audrey said as she crossed to stand in front of Meg. She raised her hands, reaching out, and Meg found herself pressing away from this woman she'd once called mother, against the cold marble of the unlit fireplace. "I've only just found my baby again. Don't spoil our reunion."

Meg lifted the cup and brought it to her lips, blocking Audrey's advance. Audrey gasped and stepped back, pulling a wounded expression across her carefully made-up face.

Meg looked longingly at the button hidden in the carved marble of the mantel. One push of that and she could be out of here, without having to say another word. But what good would that do her? No more than getting into a cat fight with Audrey or listing grievances to the three of them would. They'd hear what they wanted to hear, believe what they wanted to believe and do what they wanted to do in spite of anything she said. She'd never be able to make them see their guilt or their fault, and now she didn't want them to see their pain. It was too personal to share with three people who quite probably would only use it as a weapon in their greed and selfishness.

She slid her glance away from the button and gave the

Duke and Duchess of Windsor a silent salute as she turned
to face those who'd had her running and hiding most of her
life.

"There will be no reunion," Meg said quietly, "because
there is nothing to reunite. We all know that everything between us was based on a lie that I no longer have to live."

"Why you ungrateful little—" Audrey's face contorted
with the effort it took to control her lunging temper. "We
took you in, clothed you, educated you, put up with your
screaming nightmares and the embarrassment of your inability to function on a par with your classmates—"

And begrudged her every moment of every day, Meg
thought. Maybe a cat fight wouldn't be so bad after all. No.
She wouldn't expose herself that much. "I have questions
about my childhood," she said instead, "but I believe I will
let the FBI find answers to those questions for me."

"You've gotten pretty full of it, Meg," Blake said in the
same tone he'd once used when he challenged how she'd
spent her grocery allowance. "Are you going to use the FBI
to continue to hide my son from me?"

Don't rise to his taunts. Steeling herself, she refused to
cower or to answer questions meant only to provoke. She
did allow herself to look down at Audrey over the rim of the
china cup, and it felt good—really good. She'd be a liar if
she tried to convince herself it didn't.

"I have been in consultation with the Carlton attorneys
since my arrival in Avalon. Since my adoption was based on
a blatant lie about my identity, it is now in the process of
being voided.

"But that was not my most pressing concern."

"No, I'd imagine figuring out how to spend your windfall
would probably occupy a whole bunch of your time. Tell
me, have you had any time for our kid?"

She glanced at Blake. "Danny is twelve years old. He has
no good memories of you, but I hope for his sake you build
some with him. You will be allowed limited, supervised visitation with Danny as long as you attempt to build a father-
son relationship with him. But you will never have custody

of him. And you will never have control of any of the wealth he will one day inherit. I've seen to that—''

''Bitch!''

Meg placed her cup on the mantel and lifted trembling fingers to rest near the button. Would he hurt her? Would he dare, with witnesses in the room, and help only a few feet away? With Blake, she could never be sure.

She swept the three of them with an icy glare that hid the cowering child she had once been—still felt herself to be. ''Mr. Wilson will be arriving before nightfall with the vehicle he rented in Albuquerque—''

''Dad? My father's coming here? Why?''

Blake seemed genuinely surprised, as though he truly hadn't known, but James's reaction surpassed that. His color faded, leaving him a sick-looking gray. He turned to his wife and spoke through vocal cords made suddenly tight. ''You couldn't leave it alone, could you? Damn it, Audrey. And damn you.''

Audrey whimpered—actually whimpered. Meg looked across the room. At some point Lucas had stepped into the doorway, perhaps in response to the loud voices. His glance met hers, but he waited silently for her to continue.

''Mr. Wilson will be arriving tonight,'' she repeated. ''There is no reason for any of you to linger in Avalon after then.''

It was a perfect exit line; too bad no one but her recognized it as such. Meg felt her life spinning out of control as Audrey and Blake both advanced on her, spewing out versions of what she had already heard from them too many times in the past. She felt a hand on her shoulder and spun to find Lucas at her side.

''Miss Carlton has been a lot kinder than I would have been.'' His voice held the soft whispery quality that had entranced her so in the quiet moments of the night they had spent together. Now it held a menace she had never before felt from him. ''Mr. Huxtable has asked me to convey to you the Lodge's sincere apologies. Beginning tomorrow, all the rooms are held by prior reservations. I've taken the liberty of notifying your pilot to remain in Avalon until tomorrow to return you to Simonville. You should also be aware that there are no facilities in Avalon for the return of the rental car Mr. Wilson is bringing.''

''Damn it, Lambert. You can't do that to us. There are laws in this country—''

Lucas pinned Blake with a cool, unyielding appraisal. ''Yes,'' he said in the same soft voice. ''There are.'' He looked at Meg and she let herself get lost for just a moment in the security he offered her. ''Are you ready to leave?''

She smiled at him with the radiant, thousand-watt smile she had been working on all her adult life. With what she knew would appear casual grace, she lifted her cape from the back of the chair and swirled it around her. ''Yes.''

Lucas gave Meg the dramatic, silent exit she needed. With a quelling glance at the three unlikely compatriots, he offered her his arm, escorted her from the room and closed the door on unwelcome visitors, unanswered questions and her past. Meg felt herself slump. He tightened his hand on hers where it rested on his arm. ''Not yet,'' he said softly.

Norris Huxtable stood at the end of the hall. He glanced at Meg, who stood tall and proud in her defiant red costume, and gave her a conspiratorial and approving smile. ''They've been informed of your conflict in reservations,'' Lucas told him. ''You'll have one more guest tonight, but they'll all be leaving tomorrow.''

Meg watched the unspoken communication that passed between the two men. She didn't question it. This was Lucas's territory, not hers. But as her energy drained away, as all the taunts of her childhood and marriage she thought she could put behind her rose up to mock her, she tightened her hand on his arm. Unbelievable. He was more attuned to her than anyone, ever, had been. Her slight touch was all the signal he needed to hurry her from the Lodge and to his Land Rover. He lifted a heavy file from the seat to the floorboard and helped her into the car. She gestured without too much enthusiasm toward the minivan.

''Later,'' Lucas said. But when he rounded the car and

closed the two of them into its leather-scented comfort and privacy, he made no effort to start the engine.

"Danny..." Oh, Lord, she'd promised her son an outing in the country, and all she wanted to do now was curl up somewhere, put her mind and heart on automatic and give herself time to heal from newly opened wounds. Even knowing they would come, and why, hadn't prepared her. Even knowing that greed—only greed—had to have prompted them to seek her out hadn't kept her from wanting to hear the words—lies, yes, lies, if necessary—that would have given her the illusion that sometime in the past twenty-five years someone had found her worthy of loving.

"Danny's all right," Lucas said. "I asked Tommy to get in touch with Jamie and have her keep him company until we got through this meeting."

Meg felt tears suspiciously close to the surface and knew she couldn't let Lucas see them. He'd probably decide that responsibility for them fell somewhere in an obscure part of his job description. "Well," she said brightly—too brightly. "At least that's over now. Thank you for all of your help."

With a barely restrained violence, Lucas beat his fist against the steering wheel. He drew a deep breath and leaned his head back against the headrest. Slowly his fists opened, and he reached for her hand, enfolding it in his larger one. "I didn't want you to go through that."

"I had to."

"I guess I knew that. But I wanted to be there for you, with you..."

"Instead of me."

"Yes. That, too." He eased her hand open and smoothed it against his thigh, caressing it with a repetitive, almost unconscious, gentle stroking. "I shouldn't have left you this morning without talking to you. We had too many things unresolved between us for me to run off without a word to you."

Thank God his eyes were still closed. She turned her face to the window and looked out at the mountainside behind the Lodge. "Oh, I think we resolved everything. I told you

I loved you. You told me not to. I shouldn't have been surprised. Other than my son, no one in my memory has ever
found anything about me worthy of love. You're more honorable and more honest than those—''

With a roar he twisted around to face her. A roar? Lucas?

''Don't you ever put yourself down like that again. And
don't you dare compare me to that pack of vultures. They're
sick, Meg. And at least one of them is probably evil. But
you're out of their grasp now—you escaped them years ago,
but you haven't realized that yet. You're warm and loving,
beautiful, quick-witted, and generous, and anyone who
doesn't love you is a fool.''

Meg felt her heart contract. The words were right. If they
had been spoken without anger, if they had been spoken the
night before, they would have made her heart sing. ''And
you, Lucas? It's been only hours since you told me you
couldn't love me.''

''I told you. It's not you—it's me. I can't love you.''

She felt his hands tighten on her shoulders. Would she
bruise? Did he know he trembled? Did he know he looked
as though he had just condemned himself to a hell of his
own making?

''Then let me go.''

''I can't. Not—not until I get you through this.''

''Oh, Lucas.'' The tears didn't fall, but now her voice
broke on a sob. ''I won't be a part of your debt. I won't put
more on you than you're already carrying for God knows
how many people.''

''Is that what you think this is?''

''Isn't it? With your attitude and my history, what else
could it be?''

''Oh, hell.''

With a grind of the starter and a flagrant abuse of his well-
tuned vehicle, he roared down the private drive of the Lodge
and turned onto the highway toward the airport.

''Where are we going?''

He glanced at her but immediately returned his attention
to the road. ''A place where we can finish this discussion,''

he said. "A place where I can show you just how wrong
you are about yourself and about why I can't seem to get
out of your life. A place I should never have let you leave
this morning."

Meg sank back against the seat and let him concentrate on
the road and whatever else was driving him. She had no
doubt that Lucas Lambert had more love locked up inside of
him than anyone she had ever known. Maybe he couldn't
love her, but if what he'd done for her hadn't been prompted
by a debt too great for anyone to have to bear, he at least
cared for her. Every action since the day he'd met her proved
that. Why wouldn't he let her care for him? Why wouldn't
he let her love him?

Did she need his permission to love him?

Of course not.

But she did need courage. A lot of it. She'd always run
before. But running wasn't an option now. Not if she was
ever to have a hope of happiness. She glanced over at Lucas,
who still gripped the steering wheel with the intensity of a
haunted man. And not, she very much feared, unless she was
willing to abandon Lucas in a futile attempt to save herself.
Yes. She would definitely need courage—enough to face
knowing that she was about to make the biggest gamble of
her life and she didn't have a clue as to how to do it.

Twelve

Lucas drove to the rear of his house and parked. Meg didn't wait for him to open her door, and she didn't wait for him to finish keying in the security code on the panel inside the house.

He wanted to talk, to argue, to convince her with logic of something she would never believe.

She pushed through a swinging door and found herself in his kitchen. She was getting to know his house, the way she was getting to know him, one hidden piece at a time. Tall, white, glass-fronted cabinets, blue ceramic tile and heavy cookware slid past the edges of her consciousness as she made her way through the room.

They didn't need words. Later they would, but not now. Now, Meg had to help them find the magic they had known last night. There was truth in that magic—healing truth—for herself, and—oh, please—for Lucas.

As she started up the curved staircase she draped her cape across the teak banister that topped the half wall of the stairs. Daylight streaming through the two-story glass brick wall that defined the other side of the stairwell cast shadows across the carpeted stairs and into the rooms below. She heard Lucas calling her name but didn't stop until she reached the top. There she turned, waiting.

He found her cape, as she had meant him to, and looked up the stairwell to where she stood. She watched as he threw back his head, as if bracing for a blow, and then slowly, much too slowly, mounted the stairs. He stopped, one step below her.

"Don't do this, Meg."

Courage? Yes, she needed courage for what she was about to do; more courage than she had ever had to draw upon before. Lucas could devastate her with his rejection. Or he could heal her with his love. And if there was a loving God, she could help heal him.

She lifted her hand to his face and bent forward, brushing her lips across his. "Love me, Lucas."

She heard what sounded like a strangled moan.

"Please, Meg…"

She knew there were words she could use and emotions she could invoke that would play on his sympathies, but she wanted no ghosts from their pasts; she wanted nothing between them but the need they felt for each other. That was enough. That had to be enough. And if she was the only one to call it love—well, she knew, and one day, if she were very, very lucky, so would he.

She stepped down one stair and slid her hands behind Lucas's head, holding him to her as she whispered against his mouth, "Yes, please."

"I shouldn't." But even with his denial, he tightened his arms around her, pulling her close.

"Yes," she told him. "You should."

"You've been through too much today. You don't know what you're doing…"

"Yes." Meg pulled back slightly, wanting Lucas to see the truth in her eyes. "I do." And then she proceeded to show him that she did. She proceeded to do what she now knew no one had ever done before; she proceeded to show

Lucas Lambert, this stern and unsmiling man who had taught her the meaning of the word, how it felt to be cherished.

With a groan, he pulled away from her. He eased her hands from his neck and lowered them, and stood with his hands on her shoulders as though holding her at bay.

"You are a magnificent woman, Meg. Don't ever doubt that."

She'd lost. Had she been a fool to think she could fight his ghosts? Or merely blinded by her need? Because his ghosts were between them, stronger than Meg ever would be. But she could be strong enough not to crumble before him. She could be strong enough to show grace in defeat. She felt his hands slide down her arms, to her hands, and slowly, gently, begin unclasping fingers she didn't know she had fisted.

She lowered her eyes, damming the tears that welled in them.

"Your hands give you away every time," Lucas told her, releasing her hands to lift her chin. He stood perfectly still, letting her see the need and indecision that warred within him, letting her see the moment when the needs he had probably never admitted having, won.

Meg felt her breath catch in her throat and swayed toward him, but he caught her and swept her up into his arms.

"Lucas!" she gasped. "I'm too—"

"Hush." He refused to let her finish her denial. "We're doing this right."

She had tossed the spread over the bed before they left only hours before, not wanting to leave its rumpled disarray to gossip of the joy she had found there. Now Lucas tore it away and lowered her to the sheets that still bore the impressions and the mingled scents of that joy.

Show me what it's like to feel loved, she had asked of him, and he had. Oh, yes, he certainly had. Now it was time for her to show him. Struggling up, she stilled him with no more than a touch. His tie came first, as she loosened it, and then his jacket.

She felt the belt of her tunic give way as she eased open the first tiny shirt button.

"Damnation," he muttered, and she realized he was stymied in his efforts to free her from the tangle of their arms and what seemed like yards of silk. Laughing gently, she released her grasp on his shirt button and raised her arms, freeing him to pull tunic and turtleneck over her head.

He laughed, too, until he'd sent the flash of red silk to join his suit jacket and turned to look at her. Then his laughter silenced as he looked down at her where she had settled back against the pile of pillows. His breath caught, and he raised his hand to trace one hesitant finger across the delicate filigree of lace that barely covered her breasts before blending into the shimmer of nude colored silk.

There were certainly some advantages to this Cinderella business, Meg thought, as she remembered the utilitarian, nononsense cotton she had worn all her life.

"You are so beautiful."

Meg lifted a suddenly trembling hand to his face. *So was he in every way that counted.* But she didn't think he'd believe that. "You're repeating yourself."

"Am I?"

"Yes," she said softly. With a gentle tug, she pulled him down until his chest grazed her breasts. "Don't stop."

"No," he told her, spearing his hands into her hair to hold her still. "I won't."

His mouth took hers in a searing cry of the need he wouldn't voice, and she answered with every fiber of her being. She'd not only show him how it felt to be loved, she would love him—love him in spite of ghosts, in spite of debts, in spite of that persistent voice in the back of her mind that sounded suspiciously like Audrey and even now questioned her ability to love or be loved—love him for as long as he would let her, and maybe, for this one day at least, he would believe that she did.

And maybe, for this moment, he'd let himself love her.

It felt as though he did. Last night, his touch had been hesitant, almost reverent as he brought her to mindlessness.

Now, no less caring, he seemed…hungrier, needier, more insistent. But so was she. Cast-off silk and wool and leather gave mute witness to that need as finally she felt the length of him against her.

She turned in his arms, drawing him to her. "Lucas," she murmured. "Oh, Lucas."

Her hands found the texture of him, the warmth of him, the strength of him. Her lips, hungry, needy, and yes, insistent, nipped and tasted and teased.

Now he moaned in her arms, turning, burrowing closer, then pulling away to give her again with his hands and lips those touches of almost unbearable pleasure he had first shown her last night, touches of almost unbearable pleasure she had only dreamed could exist, until this man who swore he couldn't love had so unselfishly proven could and did exist.

But only with him, Meg knew. Only with him.

She wanted to give to him, needed to give to him, but she felt herself coming apart in his arms, as he was in hers. She heard herself murmuring his name, whimpering broken pleas. But there was no weakness in those pleas, only a strength that the two of them found as at last he joined them and once again spun her out of her body, with him, to that place where the two of them had no past, no ghosts, only a blindingly clear, bright, ecstatic present and the promise of a future filled with love.

The bedside telephone woke her—just one ring, quickly silenced when someone answered on a distant extension. She didn't need to open her eyes to know the truth. After all they had shared, Lucas had left her alone in his bed. He had covered her with a woven blanket when he left, but he had left.

Meg lifted her hands to her mouth to silence her cry of protest. His ghosts had won.

Later, showered and carefully costumed in her red silk, Meg found Lucas in the kitchen, seated at an enameled white table with the contents of a heavy file spread out around him. A cordless telephone lay beside an empty coffee cup. He had dressed, but not in one of the tailored suits she had grown accustomed to seeing him wear. He had donned a pair of comfortable cotton slacks, one of those last-century looking shirts with only the band for a collar, and a pair of moccasins. For the first time she glimpsed in him an image of how those distant ancestors of his must have looked when they met the early settlers of Avalon. He glanced up when she entered the room, and for a moment his eyes mirrored the emotion of what they had shared and what they had lost.

"I heard the telephone," she said.

"I'm sorry it woke you."

So polite. So noncommittal. "Has Blake's father arrived?"

Lucas nodded.

The sunlight slanting through the high windows told her that church had probably been over for hours. "I'd better call Danny. He'll be worried."

Lucas handed her the phone, and she punched out the number. Mrs. Tompkins answered, and Meg heard the spat of computer-generated laser fire and exploding objects before Danny mumbled into the telephone.

"Did you see Dad?"

"Yes, Danny, I did."

"So when do we leave?"

Meg closed her eyes against the pain in her son's voice. "Oh, honey," she said. "We don't. This time he leaves."

"Are you okay?"

Yes, she was. But was her son? Would he ever be? "Yes. You know I love you."

"Yeah, Ma. I know. Me, too." She heard what sounded suspiciously like a sniffle. "So I guess this means he screwed up our plans to go to the ranch."

"Danny, it wasn't all his fault—"

"Yeah. Mom, don't try to tell me how much he really loves me. We both know he doesn't. It's okay. I'm used to . I'm just sick and tired of him spoiling everything."

"He won't," Meg promised. "Not ever again."

Lucas glanced sharply at her, and Meg realized that tears had spilled from her eyes and drenched her cheeks.

Danny mumbled something about Jamie and a computer game, and somehow Meg managed to end her call on an upbeat and switch off the phone. When Lucas wrapped her in his arms, she had no reserves left to fight the despair that swamped her. Never enough. Her love was never enough. Not for James and Audrey. Not for Blake. Not for Lucas. And now, it seemed, it had never been enough for Danny, either.

He pressed her face against his throat and held her, rocking her gently until she reached within herself for one last particle of strength. Danny wasn't the parents who had betrayed her. Lucas wasn't Blake.

And she wasn't that skinny, long-legged, awkward, too-young child who had all but begged for someone to love her—for someone to accept her love. No one had, then. But now her son did love her. Her new family would. And if Lucas couldn't, that didn't demean the love she felt for him.

She eased herself away from the too tempting warmth of him, and almost reluctantly he let her go. She gestured to the table and the naggingly familiar-looking file. "What are you working on? It looks impressive."

Lucas grimaced. He opened a cabinet door and retrieved a cup, which he filled from the half-full coffeepot and handed to her. When he didn't answer, Meg set the cup aside. A red and white chef's apron hung from a peg near the stove. From its size, it was clearly Lucas's, but it seemed far out of character for the man who now stood beside the table, tracing his fingers along a long, slender pen that lay on a pile of documents.

Whatever it was, was important, and she knew by his silence that it probably related to her.

She lifted the apron from the peg and tied it around her. "Okay, let me try another question. I'm starving. What do you have that I can fix for lunch?"

His eyes pinned her with knowledge of her lie. "Meg, s

down for a moment. Please. I have to ask you some questions.''

A cup had worked as defense against Audrey; maybe an ironstone mug would ward off the menace she suddenly sensed hovering all around her. It was worth a try. She lifted her cup and held it in both hands, but she didn't sit.

''What kind of questions?''

''This is the file on your family's kidnapping.''

Meg felt for the support of the cabinet behind her.

''Paul Slater called earlier with some information I had requested. Tell me what you know about Blake's father.''

Meg studied him across the width of the kitchen. Blake's father? Where was he going with this? ''Very little. He's a bully. He terrified me, but I did my best not to let him know. After the time Blake dragged me to his house to meet him, I stayed away from him, and he stayed away from me. He was as against the marriage as Audrey and James were. I don't have the slightest idea why he came to Avalon.''

''When did you meet him?''

''The day Blake and I got married.''

''Not before?''

Meg coughed out a rueful chuckle. ''I think if I had met him before, I might have given more thought to marrying a man who looked so much like him. Who turned out to be so much like him.''

''You don't remember him ever being at the Stemples's home?''

She shook her head. ''No. My impression was they didn't know each other. Why, Lucas?''

''Connections. Connections that shouldn't be, but are. Blake isn't the only one who took a leave of absence from the Simonville PD. His father did, almost thirty years ago. He left wife and child in Simonville, while he took a job with the Sacramento PD and a part-time job, even though he didn't seem to need the money, as a private security guard. James was in the state legislature at the time. He and Audrey lived in Sacramento while the legislature was in session.''

"Coincidence?" Meg asked. "Sacramento's close, and big enough so that they might not have met."

"Oh, they met," Lucas told her. "I just don't know when or how, yet, but I will find out. Because the part-time job he took was with Carlton Enterprises, and the person who hired him was your uncle, the one who became Edward's guardian."

The mug slipped from her hands and shattered on the tile floor, splattering coffee and shards of crockery.

Lucas was at her side before the last shard stopped spinning.

"What are you saying?"

"I'm only asking, Meg, asking questions that should have been asked years ago but weren't."

"No." The implications of what he had just said were too horrible to bear. "No, I don't want to know this. It's ancient history, Lucas. Let it stay in the past."

"I can't, Meg. I can't. I have to do this. For Edward. But most of all for you."

"For me? If you're doing it for me, I want you to quit. I don't want to know. I don't want to know."

"Meg." She felt his hands on her arms, holding her as her emotions threatened to spin out of control. "Don't you see? All I've done since the day we met is take from you. I have to learn who robbed you of your childhood. It's the only thing I can give you in return."

"Oh, you idiot!" Meg lowered her head to his shoulder and sobbed once before jerking upright. "Don't you know? Can't you believe me? I love you. And you don't measure love on a balance sheet. You don't *take* love. If you could, I'd have been the best-loved child in the world. And so would you. It's a gift, Lucas." Where had they come from, these words she heard herself shouting at him, these words that for the first time she understood? "It's a gift freely given," she said on a whisper. "You can only accept it if it's offered, or mourn for it if it isn't."

She looked at him in silence while her words echoed around them. For a moment, as he lifted his hand toward her, she thought he might take her in his arms, but instead he dropped his hand to his side, fisting it, as she too often did.

"I want to go home," she said suddenly. "I want to see Danny. I don't want him out of my sight until you ask and answer all your questions and those people are out of Avalon."

His mobile phone rang just as Lucas braked to a stop in front of the gates to Edward's house. With a grimace and a quick glance at her, Lucas answered its indecently cheerful summons. Even from across the seat, Meg recognized the panic in Jamie's voice through the tiny speaker, but her words were indistinct.

Lucas had remained silent on their drive from his house. Even through the turmoil of emotions his latest disclosure had spawned, Meg sensed him drawing his defenses around him, rebuilding any chinks in the professional, unfeeling facade he presented to the world. Now, as he listened to his daughter's frantic call, he became even more the harsh and unyielding man.

"Calm down," he said, letting none of that harshness creep into his voice as he talked with his daughter. "We're here now. Tell Tommy to let us in.

"No. I know you wouldn't do that." The gates swung open, and Lucas drove through. He never paused in his soft reassurances to his daughter, but his wary glance swept the tree-bordered driveway and surrounding grounds. "I know, Jamie. It isn't your fault. No one will blame you."

How could he be so gentle with Jamie—with her, with Danny, with Marianna, and with God alone knew how many others—and so unforgiving with himself? And what could Jamie have done that was so bad she felt she had to beg her father's forgiveness?

Lucas braked to a stop beneath the porte cochere. "We're here," he said. "Tell Tommy to contact Tully. Yes, I will." His hand tightened on the receiver. "Just as soon as I hang up. Yes. I love you, too."

Lucas set the phone back in its cradle and turned to Meg.

"What is it?" she asked.

He reached for her hands and held them in a clasp just short of painful. A cold knot of dread seemed to reach from him to her, and she knew an anxiety her new life in Avalon had lured her into believing she'd never again have to feel.

"Danny?" she asked through a throat too tight to permit more than a whisper. She tried to pull her hands away—she had to get to her son—but he held her with implacable strength. "What's happened to Danny?"

"Nothing," he said. She wanted to believe him so badly that for a moment she did. "Jamie just...can't find him."

"What!"

"He wanted to go outside," Lucas told her. "Jamie said he was really angry—at his father, not you," he added as quickly as the question formed in her mind. "She agreed to go out, as long as they stayed on the estate grounds. They were playing an improvised game of catch as Danny vented some of his anger. He lobbed a ball past her into the shrubbery, and when she found it and returned, he wasn't there."

Meg stared at him in mute silence, fighting the whimper that threatened her.

"He'll be all right," Lucas promised, lifting her hands to hold them against his chest. He would have pulled her to him, Meg knew, but she stiffened, resisting the temporary caring that was all he could offer her. "He *is* all right. He has to be somewhere on the grounds. He just doesn't want to be found."

"Danny doesn't sulk—"

"Meg."

"Usually," she amended, remembering the sulking he had done since their arrival in Avalon. "But he's never hidden from a problem, Lucas. Except when I forced him to."

The house door slammed open, and Jamie ran out to meet them. Reluctantly Lucas released Meg's hands, opened his door and caught his daughter in the comforting embrace Meg had refused.

Danny wasn't on the grounds or in the house. Half an hour later, after all of Edward's security people and half of the staff of Lucas's well-equipped department had scoured every inch of the estate, Meg knew that Lucas had to accept what she had told him: Danny didn't hide.

She'd shed the red silk in favor of something more practical for searching—her past-life no-nonsense jeans, sneakers and a sweatshirt. She'd been over the grounds too many times to count, and had called until her voice was hoarse. The last time she'd seen Lucas, he'd been in huddled conference with Tully and Mrs. Tompkins. Now she heard his voice raised in a shout, and Tully's answering call and followed their voices to an ivy-covered corner in the back wall. Lucas stood away from it as he and Tully studied the ground. He stopped her when she drew near.

She saw what he studied—a jumble of trampled plants at the base of the wall, and sporadic broken vines on the way up and over the ancient brick that guarded the rear of Edward's impenetrable estate.

"I think this is where he left the grounds."

"Or was taken?" Meg asked.

Tully glanced away, unable to meet her eyes, but Lucas didn't flinch. "I don't think that happened—there isn't any sign of the struggle your son would have put up—but I can't tell you definitely that he left on his own. Or where he is."

"But we both know where to look for answers, don't we?" God. Would Meg never be free of them? Had she let them ruin—helped them ruin—her son's life, the way they had ruined hers?

"Get someone on the other side of this wall," Lucas said to Tully. "See if you can pick up his trail. Where are the dogs?"

"On the way," Tully told him. "I sent for them as soon as I got Tommy's call."

"Good," Lucas said, nodding. "Good." He took Meg's hand and pulled her away from the wall. "Let us do our job, Meg. Please. I promise to bring him back to you."

"The Lodge." Meg refused to be distracted from what she knew to be the truth. "He's either gone there to confront his father, or someone—one of them—knows where he is."

"They're under surveillance, Meg. All of them. They have been since before they set foot in this jurisdiction."

"So was Danny," she spat out.

Lucas released her and stepped away. "Yes. He was."

"Oh, Lucas." Meg wanted to call back her words—she'd never meant to attack him. With his ingrained sense of honor and responsibility, he had to be assuming all responsibility for her son's disappearance. "I'm so sorry."

"So am I." He glanced over her shoulder and, with a nod of his head, urged someone to step forward. "Take her back to the house, Tommy. I have a search to see to."

Meg had stolen his car; while he'd been coordinating the search that would bring her son back to her, Meg had slipped into his Land Rover and abandoned the safety of her home as quickly and efficiently as her twelve-year-old escape-artist son had. And no one even suspected she was not where she had told Tommy she would be, upstairs in her room resting—*resting?* Meg?—until he had prepared to leave to check out the one viable lead he had on Danny's whereabouts.

Lucas stormed downstairs from Meg's room, where his daughter lay lost in exhausted sleep on Meg's bed, and did his best to ignore Tommy's raised eyebrow at his uncharacteristic lack of composure. He commandeered one of his seasoned deputies and put him in charge of the search before he entrusted Tully with the task that he knew would return Meg's son to her.

"Take me to the Lodge," he ordered Tommy. He saw her lips quirk in the grin she'd finally lost the battle to restrain. "Damn it, Tommy. It isn't funny."

Her smile immediately faded. "Is Meg in danger?"

"I don't know," Lucas said. "There's a wild card there. I just don't know which one it is. And I don't know how any of them will react if she charges in, accusing them of taking Danny."

Norris met her at the door. She should have suspected Lucas had warned him of her arrival when he met her, or even when he showed her into the same lovely sitting room she had used earlier that day and left her to wait while he summoned his guests. She should have suspected, but she didn't. Instead she waited. And waited. Until the door opened, and she whirled around from her vigil at the mantel to see Lucas and Tommy enter the room.

"Are you out of your mind?" Lucas asked.

"He's my son. What do you expect me to do?"

Tommy stepped back into the hallway and closed the door, leaving the two of them alone in the room.

"I expect you to let me do my job, Meg. You may not believe it now, but I'm good at what I do. Danny isn't here, and I don't think any of these people know where he is—"

"You can't be sure of that."

"—but if he were, do you have any idea of the harm you could have done by bursting in here with accusations?"

"At least ask them if they've stolen my son. You can't let them get off scot-free. You have to at least ask them, Lucas."

He crossed the room and gripped her shoulders in his hands. "Why, Meg?" He held her immobile as he searched her eyes with questions that were frightening in their intensity.

"Because I—" *Because why?* A truth lingered somewhere in her words, somewhere in her actions, but it eluded her as surely as the words she had started to speak. She studied each familiar harsh feature of Lucas's face before once again meeting his eyes and praying that their perception might find it for her. No. They still held only questions. And the soul-deep loneliness she had thought, hoped, prayed never to see there again. "I don't know."

He continued to hold her for a second, two, three, before releasing her and stepping back so that he in no way touched her, not even with the energy that pulsed from his body.

"Yes," he said. "I'll question them. It's time. But I want you to stay here while I do it."

Meg sagged in relief. "Yes. I want to be with you when—"

He shook his head. "No, Meg. Here. In this room. Away from them. I don't want you ever to have to face them again."

Oh, Lucas. He was still protecting her. She suspected he always would. But from what? "Don't you know me at all?" she asked. "I've run and hidden from these people all my life. I can't do that anymore. I won't do that anymore."

He remained silent for a moment, and she sensed he was gathering arguments to use against her. But then, surprising her, he nodded abruptly. "All right. But if you can't promise me that you will let me ask the questions and let me do all the talking, I swear I will lock you in this room."

Meg felt questions of her own battering to be asked. Why? Why if he thought they had nothing to do with Danny's disappearance was he so concerned? Why did it feel as though he were again protecting her from danger? Why did she feel again the need in him to hold her—a need she knew he would not act upon, might never again act upon. She glanced up the scant inches that separated them and saw the resolve in his eyes. Regardless of his reasons, he meant what he said. And did she really need to know his reasons? Lucas was never arbitrary. It seemed it all came down to trust. And if she knew nothing else in this new life of hers, she knew she could trust Lucas Lambert. With her life. Even with her son's. "You have my promise."

Norris had gathered them all in a small conference room only a short distance down the hall. Two deputies waited outside. Meg didn't understand the need for them, but she said nothing as she entered the room between Lucas and Tommy. While Tommy stayed behind to close the door and take a position near it, Meg followed Lucas across the room to where her one-time family sat in a grouping of comfortable upholstered chairs.

Blake's father saw them first and stood. A chill shuddered through Meg as she saw that he was in his blue uniform. Why? And just as quickly she had the answer. The unofficial fraternity. For some reason he felt a need for all the influence he could demand, regardless of how blatantly he demanded it. Blake rose, too, and whispered something to his father.

Lucas ignored all of them until he had taken a position at the inevitable fireplace. Meg stood a few feet away from him, giving him the floor but remaining far away from the others.

Her father-in-law cast a quick glance at her before turning his attention to Lucas. "Sheriff Lambert. Perhaps now we can get your deputy straightened out. He had the audacity to demand my sidearm." He stepped forward, hand extended. "It's good to meet you."

Lucas ignored his hand. "It probably isn't," he said with enough contempt in his lazy drawl to stop the man's approach. "Danny Wilson is missing."

Blake's head jerked up. "You can't possibly think any of us had anything to do with it. We've been locked up in this high-class jail of yours since the moment we arrived. The kid's probably just off doing whatever the hell she's been letting him get away with all of his life. I've told her time after time he needed discipline."

Let me do all the talking. Only her promise to Lucas kept Meg quiet. But then Lucas said most of what she would have.

"I find your concern for your missing son touching, Mr. Wilson. But after reading numerous medical reports that familiarized me with your idea of discipline, I'm not too surprised."

"Wait a minute—"

"Please be seated," Lucas said with a steely quiet that would have had her looking for the nearest chair. "Please," he repeated. "Be seated."

Blake at last returned to his chair; his father, however, stepped behind his and rested his hands on its back.

"What's this all about?" Audrey asked, but she sank back in the chair after James put a restraining hand on her arm.

Lucas stretched one arm out across the mantel, and Meg wondered if a bell were hidden in this one, too, before turning to her with what she would have sworn was an apology in his eyes. Too soon he broke that fragile contact and gave his attention to the four in front of him. "No," he said. "I don't think you are responsible, directly, for Danny's absence. However, Miss Carlton isn't so sure."

For some reason most of Lucas's attention seemed focused on Blake's father, and against her will, Meg found herself watching him, too. He'd worn his uniform the last time she'd seen him, and then, as now, he exuded an aura of menace—an aura no one but her seemed to sense. Before, she had been too stunned even to react to his antagonism. Now she had time to question it.

It's a policeman, Edward. Maybe he'll know what happened to the phone lines.

Meg blinked. The voice had been faint, but distinct, softly lilting, feminine, struggling up from the shadows of her past.

"It's amazing what seemingly innocent coincidences can do when a person's been deeply and actively involved in recalling old memories."

She glanced sharply at Lucas. What was he saying?

"Especially if they, at least superficially, parallel some of those memories."

Audrey whimpered.

"Be quiet, woman." But this time the admonition came not from James but from Blake's father.

Be quiet, damn it! I don't want to have to hurt you.

His voice. But not his voice.

Can't you keep her quiet? I've got a houseful of people downstairs.

"You—" Meg caught her hand to her mouth. Had she actually spoken? She didn't think so. *Let me do all the talking.* Yes. Yes, she would let him do that. But about something else, Lucas. Please. About something else.

A soft knock sounded at the door, and Tommy moved to open it. From where she stood, Meg saw Tully and the other deputies in the hallway, behind the small sturdy figure who held her attention.

"Danny," she cried out. "Oh, thank God."

He grinned and waved, then, sure of his welcome, and pushed past Tommy. With a glance at Lucas, who gave a violent shake of his head, Tommy reached for his arm, but Danny evaded her and ran into the room.

"Danny." Lucas's voice stopped him. "This is not a good time. Please leave the room. Your mother will be with you in a minute. Meg?"

Meg looked from her son to Lucas, but Lucas didn't notice. His attention was focused entirely on the older Wilson. And *his* attention was completely on Meg.

She had spoken. But what had it meant? Whatever it was, her son needed to leave. Now. "Please, Danny. Go to Tully."

"And leave you here with him?" Danny jerked a thumb in the direction of his father. "No way, Ma. If anyone leaves, it's gonna be him. I decided that on my way out to the ranch. If Tully hadn't come for me, I'd have been on my way here, anyway. We're through running."

Blake's father had moved. When? But now he stood closer to Danny. Visibly closer. And he took another step. And another. But he wasn't the only one moving. Lucas, and Tommy, too, stepped forward. But not soon enough. She saw a blue-uniformed arm reach out and snatch her son's arm.

"No," she cried, not knowing where the terror came from, but feeling it permeate her every cell. She lunged forward, but Tommy was there, yanking on that horrid blue-clad arm, shoving Danny away. She'd seen this before. All of it. When? Where? "No," she moaned. And then she was running, pummeling him as she knew she had before. "You won't hurt her again!" she cried. "You won't. You won't. You won't."

She was still out.

Lucas eased himself onto the sofa by her side and took Meg's hand in his, chafing it, willing her back to consciousness. He'd carried her to this room too long ago now for him to think this no more than a simple faint. And yet, if he truly remembered all he suspected she had, she'd need the blessing of unconsciousness to help her deal with the shock of remembering.

Finally her head moved, and her lashes fluttered.

"Meg." He summoned her back to him. She opened her eyes and smiled at him. "Did you kiss me awake?" Her brow furrowed. "No. Why do I keep wandering into the wrong fairy tale? I'm Cinderella, not Sleeping Beauty."

Oh, she was going to hate herself when she remembered this conversation. "I have someone here who needs to talk to you. Are you awake enough yet?"

She shook her head, a tiny little shake, to clear it, and opened her eyes fully. "Lucas?" But the boy standing guard behind him had waited long enough. He pushed between Lucas and Meg. "Danny?"

"Gee, Ma, why'd you have to go and get all goofy on me. I'm all right. Are you all right? Gee. You missed everything. Tommy took him out. I mean, I thought Jamie was good, but Mrs. Tompkins is really something. *Are you all right?*"

Meg lifted her hand and touched his face. Yes. She was. And so was he. "I love you, squirt. Have I told you that today?"

Danny grimaced but endured her caress. "Yeah. But... You never faint." He glared at Lucas before turning back to his mother. "You're not—you know, pregnant or anything, are you?"

Lucas heard a discreet cough behind him, thankful he'd assigned Tommy the task of watching over Danny and not Tully or one of the hotel staff. Meg looked up at him. Yes she was definitely going to hate just about everything said in this room so far. But maybe that would take her mind off the other, darker things, she had learned today.

"No, Danny, I'm not," she said. She smiled, then, taking all threat out of her words. "But what I am is real concerned about what you're learning in school. Do you think I ought to pay a visit to your teachers?"

"Danny?" Tommy spoke up from behind them. "We need to let them talk now. Your mother needs to know what's happening."

Lucas suspected that only Danny's new respect for

Tommy made him answer her summons, but he did, after leaning forward and bussing an embarrassed and awkward kiss on his mother's cheek. "You take care of her," he ordered.

"I will," Lucas promised him.

Danny squared his shoulders and hesitated before sticking out his hand. Surprised, and flattered beyond words, Lucas accepted Danny's handshake. "See that you do," Danny told him before spinning on his heel and marching from the room with an amused Tommy following closely behind.

Meg struggled to rise. Lucas helped her with an arm behind her. Still dizzy, she leaned against the sofa and studied him with wary eyes. "What just happened between you and my son?"

Lucas smiled and brushed a curl from her cheek. "I think he just gave you into my keeping."

"But you don't want me."

He leaned forward, resting his elbows on his knees and grasping his hands as he sought words that would convince her he did. Why should they be so hard to find, when the others, the ones to drive her away, had clamored to be spoken.

"Audrey is singing," he told her. "She began talking so fast we barely had a chance to read her her rights. She's putting the blame on anyone she can think of, but she's spilling dates and dollars and names. It might have been her idea to begin with, but James supplied the money when Wilson brought you to them. It seems they were all involved, except Blake." This much he could give her, and her son. "Danny's father never knew."

Meg closed her eyes. "It wasn't a nightmare," she said, and he knew she was remembering again. "No wonder I couldn't go behind it."

"No. It wasn't a nightmare. You'd probably just seen your parents murdered when he brought you to the Stemples's house."

"Why?"

He hated the lost sound in her voice but knew she had to

ask. "A failing marriage, James's sagging career and an extra twenty-five thousand dollars."

"For my whole family?"

"No." He turned to her and reached for her hands. She held onto him as shudders racked her body. "No. That was his first job. Selling you was a bonus for him. We may never prove it, but I think that he was hired by your uncle to either kidnap for ransom or kill your family—"

"He was in uniform."

"That explains how he got close, then." To hell with it. He took Meg in his arms and held her against his chest. "You were supposed to die, Meg."

She tangled her hands in his shirt and held tightly but made no sound.

Words. Never had he needed them so badly. Words to explain what he had felt when he caught her in his arms. Words to explain what he had felt when he learned how close she had come to death. Words to explain why he now knew he didn't have to let her go.

"You were supposed to die. It's a miracle that you didn't. I was supposed to die. Another miracle."

He tucked her head under his chin and rocked her. "Edward told me something I'm only now beginning to understand. He said that nothing in his control brought Jennie into his life but he wasn't going to turn down the gift of a miracle. He hadn't believed in them, you see. Never had. And neither had I.

"Between us, you and I have at least three miracles—our lives and the love we feel for each other."

She tensed, and he sensed her drawing away from him. As he had withdrawn from her too many times in the past? He soothed a hand over her back and held her firmly in place. He couldn't let her go. Not until she heard him out.

"I thought I could leave you," he said. "I thought there would come a time, soon, when you would no longer need me. That's not going to happen, Meg. You need me to give you my love. You need me to accept the love you give me. Why was that so hard for me to understand?"

She shook her head against his chest. "Oh, Lucas." She pushed away from him. He didn't hold her. Holding her would do no good if she wanted to go.

She took his face in her hands.

"And your debt?" she asked.

His debt. Something else he had not understood until today. "Gifts, Meg. Our lives were gifts.

"You told me today that you can't take love, you can only accept it if it's freely given."

She didn't move; she didn't speak. Lucas fought a rising panic. Had he driven her away?

"Until I met you, I thought that loving and being loved was an act of selfishness. I couldn't see that those people in the village had given me the ultimate act of love, and there was not one act of selfishness in it. I couldn't see that there is no debt too great when one values and honors the gift that created it."

Tears welled in Meg's eyes. "And my gift, Lucas?"

The moment of truth. He hadn't felt such fear since waiting wounded in a cave for the gunmen to find him. But she deserved his honesty. "I'll accept it—I'll cherish it, if it's given," he told her, "and I'll mourn the rest of my life if it's not."

Meg drew a deep quavering breath and closed her eyes briefly, only to open them and show him a wealth of love waiting there for him. Oh, yes. For him.

She leaned forward and brushed her lips across his. "Don't mourn, my love," she said as she moved closer and slid her arms around him to hold him to her. "Don't mourn."

* * * * *

Don't miss Silhouette's newest cross-line promotion

Five stellar authors, five evocative stories, five fabulous Silhouette series— pregnant mom on the run!

October 1998: THE RANCHER AND THE AMNESIAC BRIDE
by top-notch talent **Joan Elliott Pickart**
(Special Edition)

November 1998: THE DADDY AND THE BABY DOCTOR
by Romance favorite **Kristin Morgan** (Romance)

December 1998: THE SHERIFF AND THE IMPOSTOR BRIDE
by award-winning author **Elizabeth Bevarly** (Desire)

January 1999: THE MILLIONAIRE AND THE PREGNANT PAUPER
by rising star **Christie Ridgway** (Yours Truly)

February 1999: THE MERCENARY AND THE NEW MOM by *USA Today* bestselling author **Merline Lovelace** (Intimate Moments)

Only in—

Silhouette Books

Available at your favorite retail outlet.

Look us up on-line at: http://www.romance.net   SSEFTB

Take 2 bestselling love stories FREE

Plus get a FREE surprise gift!

Special Limited-Time Offer

Mail to Silhouette Reader Service™

3010 Walden Avenue
P.O. Box 1867
Buffalo, N.Y. 14240-1867

YES! Please send me 2 free Silhouette Desire® novels and my free surprise gift. Then send me 6 brand-new novels every month, which I will receive months before they appear in bookstores. Bill me at the low price of $3.12 each plus 25¢ delivery and applicable sales tax, if any.* That's the complete price, and a saving of over 10% off the cover prices—quite a bargain! I understand that accepting the books and gift places me under no obligation ever to buy any books. I can always return a shipment and cancel at any time. Even if I never buy another book from Silhouette, the 2 free books and the surprise gift are mine to keep forever.

225 SEN CH7U

Name	(PLEASE PRINT)	
Address	Apt. No.	
City	State	Zip

This offer is limited to one order per household and not valid to present Silhouette Desire® subscribers. *Terms and prices are subject to change without notice.
Sales tax applicable in N.Y.

UDES-98

©1990 Harlequin Enterprises Limited

The World's Most Eligible Bachelors are about to be named! And Silhouette Books brings them to you in an all-new, original series....

World's Most Eligible Bachelors

Twelve of the sexiest, most sought-after men share every intimate detail of their lives in twelve never-before-published novels by the genre's top authors.

Don't miss these unforgettable stories by:

Dixie Browning

MARIE FERRARELLA

Jackie Merritt

Tracy Sinclair

BJ James

RACHEL LEE

Suzanne Carey

Gina Wilkins

VICTORIA PADE

MAGGIE SHAYNE

Anne McAllister

Susan Mallery

Look for one new book each month in the **World's Most Eligible Bachelors** series beginning September 1998 from Silhouette Books.

Silhouette®

Available at your favorite retail outlet.

Look us up on-line at: http://www.romance.net   PSWMEB

MATERNITY LEAVE

Coming September 1998

Three delightful stories about the blessings
and surprises of "Labor" Day.

TABLOID BABY by Candace Camp

She was whisked to the hospital in the nick of time....

THE NINE-MONTH KNIGHT
by Cait London

A down-on-her-luck secretary is experiencing
odd little midnight cravings....

THE PATERNITY TEST by Sherryl Woods

The stick turned blue before her
biological clock struck twelve....

*These three special women are very pregnant...and very
single, although they won't be either for too much longer,
because baby—and Daddy—are on their way!*

Available at your favorite retail outlet.

Look us up on-line at: http://www.romance.net   PSMATLEV

Looking For More Romance?

Visit Romance.net

Look us up on-line at: http://www.romance.net

Check in daily for these and other exciting features:

Hot off the press

View all current titles, and purchase them on-line.

What do the stars have in store for you?

Horoscope

Hot deals

Exclusive offers available only at Romance.net

Plus, don't miss our interactive quizzes, contests and bonus gifts.

PWEB

In **July 1998** comes

THE MACKENZIE FAMILY

by *New York Times* bestselling author

LINDA HOWARD

The dynasty continues with:

Mackenzie's Pleasure: Rescuing a pampered ambassador's daughter from her terrorist kidnappers was a piece of cake for navy SEAL Zane Mackenzie. It was only afterward, when they were alone together, that the real danger began....

Mackenzie's Magic: Talented trainer Maris Mackenzie was wanted for horse theft, but with no memory, she had little chance of proving her innocence or eluding the real villains. Her only hope for salvation? The stranger in her bed.

Available this July for the first time ever in a two-in-one trade-size edition. Fall in love with the Mackenzies for the first time—or all over again!

Available at your favorite retail outlet.

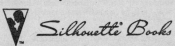

Catch more great
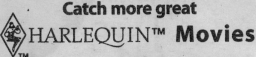
HARLEQUIN™ Movies
featured on the movie channel tmc

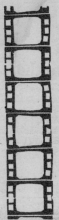

Premiering June 13th
Diamond Girl

based on the novel by bestselling
author Diana Palmer

Don't miss next month's movie!
Premiering July 11th
Another Woman
starring Justine Bateman and
Peter Outerbridge
based on the novel by Margot Dalton

If you are not currently a subscriber to
The Movie Channel, simply call your
local cable or satellite provider for more
details. Call today, and don't miss out
on the romance!

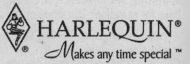

100% pure movies.
100% pure fun.

HARLEQUIN®
Makes any time special ™

Harlequin, Joey Device, Makes any time special and Superromance are trademarks of
Harlequin Enterprises Limited. The Movie Channel is a service mark of Showtime Networks, Inc.,
a Viacom Company.

An Alliance Television Production

PHMBPA698